THE PRECARIOUS ROAD
TO STARTING ANEW

by TJ Meadows

seven stories.seven weeks.seven brothers

ISBN: 978-1-949326-03-1 (eBook)

ISBN: 978-1-949326-05-5 (Hardcover)

ISBN: 978-1-949326-04-8 (Paperback)

Library of Congress Control Number: 2019935900

Any reference to historical events, real people, or real places are used fictitiously. Names, characters, and places are products of the author's imagination.

Front cover image by TJ Meadows

Editing by Lisa J. Binion

Icons by Flaticon

First printing edition 2019

www.signalhillpublishing.com

Other books by TJ Meadows:

<u>The Roads Collection</u>

The Perilous Road to Happiness

Coming Soon:

<u>The Roads Collection</u>

The Sordid Road to Rhapsody

The Treacherous Road to Rescue

<u>The Cookes of Collingswood Series</u>

A Delicate Strength

DEDICATION

Being that this is a book about brothers, it feels right to dedicate this to my own brother. I am lucky in that he happens to be one of my favorite people. He is wise and kind, reliable and smart, and maybe most important, one of my closest friends. Many thanks to him for his constant support and guidance.

Disclaimer:

Some of the characters in this book talk about medical and holistic treatments for a variety of ailments, both human and animal. They are made-up people who have no medical training. As an author, I have no medical training either, so the things you read should not be taken as medical advice. Always consult a physician or a veterinarian for any medical issues for yourself or your pets.

JACK

Retirement

Jack Cooke looked around his back yard with a smile. The people he cared about most in the world were all present to celebrate his retirement from the military. His noisy, nosey family—his parents and six brothers, their spouses and kids—had all made it for the party. His closest friends from Charleston—Lincoln and Clio, Jae, Mac, and Trey—were all there as well. The only one from that group who was missing was Becks, who was deployed in the Middle East.

Four years ago, he had met Clio on a flight to Germany as she traveled to check on Lincoln and Becks after they were injured in Afghanistan. Over the years, Jack had developed close ties to the whole group in Charleston, particularly Lincoln, who was now one of his closest friends.

Jack had retired after twenty-five years as a flight surgeon in the Air Force and bought an eighty-acre ranch just outside of the small town of Collingswood, Kentucky. He had also purchased the small town's medical practice from the retiring Dr. James Wilson. His plans were falling into place.

Jack went into the kitchen to check on Jae and Clio. They were both whipping up delicious food and sending it out the door to feed the masses. They had recruited Waverly, Jack's sister-in-law, to help. "How long until you three can call this quits and enjoy yourselves?" Jack asked as he popped a shrimp into his mouth.

"Soon," Jae said, using the whisk in a furious motion in a metal bowl. Jack put his arm around Waverly's shoulders, giving her an affectionate squeeze.

"It's really great to see you," he said. Waverly smiled and kissed his cheek.

"You need to end this, Jack. Now that you two are living in the same town you have to come to some sort of resolution," she said. Jack sighed as he walked back to the yard. He knew she was right, but he didn't know how to fix the decade-and-a-half rift between him and his eldest brother.

After grabbing a beer from the cooler, he walked to the back yard and found Lincoln sitting on a bench chatting with Mac and his brother Gavin. "Hey," he said as he sat next to them.

"Hi," Linc said, "we were just chatting about the gallery. Gavin got a new art museum project, and he was picking our brains."

Jack smiled. "Sounds like things are going well for you, Gavin." The two brothers were a year apart in age with Jack being older. In fact, there was just over four years separating the four eldest Cooke brothers. Growing up so close together seemed to amp up the emotional component of the brotherly relationships. Either they got along well, or they didn't, and there wasn't much in-between. Jack and Gavin were good. They didn't talk all that often or see each other much with Gavin living in Chicago, but there was no baggage to speak of. At least in Jack's mind.

Jack glanced across the yard, thinking how strange it was to see his brother Chance there. Chance was the eldest, two years older than Jack, and things had been strained between the two since their service together overseas. All seven of the Cooke brothers had served in the military at some point. Jack was the only one to make it a career.

"Excuse me for a second," Jack said as he stood. "Shiloh!" he called. Shiloh Warner was the new veterinarian in town. Her clinic was next door to Jack's medical office. "You made it!" he said with a smile.

"I did. Thanks again for the invite. Wow, there are a lot of people here."

"Yeah, and most of them are related to me in some way," he said, smiling. "Let me introduce you." Jack led her to a group of three men who were talking and laughing. "Shiloh, these are my younger brothers, Drew, Jakob, and Owen. Guys, this is Shiloh Warner. She is the new vet in town, and we are work neighbors."

"It's nice to meet you," Shiloh said, shyly.

"My other brother Gavin is over there on the bench, and those two over by the barn are my older brothers Chance and Pax," Jack said.

"There will be a quiz at the end of the evening," Owen joked. Shiloh smiled. Jack continued to introduce Shiloh to Lincoln; Clio, who was circulating a tray of appetizers; and Mac. As they chatted, Jack noticed Jakob intently watching Shiloh from afar as she mingled with the crowd.

It was then that Jack saw her. His heart skipped a beat. He excused himself and went to greet her. "Keri! It's so great to see you! You look stunning!" Jack was practically gushing. Keri Layton, formerly Keri Cooke, was Jack's ex-wife. He hadn't seen her in several years. "Where's Jagger?" Jagger Allenson was Keri's boyfriend. The two were not married but had been together for eight years.

"He had to work. He sends his regards." Jack knew that was a lie. Jagger hated him and would be quite content if Keri never spoke to or saw him again. Jack and Keri married young and she just wasn't cut out to be a military wife, especially with someone as dedicated to the mission as Jack. The marriage lasted about two years, but in actuality, they were only together for six or eight months of that time. Jack was in training or deployed and Keri did not do well with his constant absence. The secret Jack had been hiding was that he still loved Keri. He had barely dated during his time in the military. He used the excuse that he was married to the mission, but the reality of it was that he never wanted anyone else. He regretted that he couldn't make things work with her.

Keri felt almost exactly the same way. Thoughts of how handsome Jack was raced through her head. Deep down, if she allowed herself to admit it, she still had feelings for him too, but the hurt from losing him lay buried deep inside her. Their divorce had left her heartbroken. She wasn't sure she was over it and seeing Jack stirred up a slew of emotions that had been dormant for years.

"I wasn't sure you were going to make it," he said.

"I wasn't sure I should."

They were interrupted by Kat Bastian, the postmistress and town hypochondriac. "Dr. Cooke, I've got this terrible pain in my leg . . . " Keri smiled as she excused herself.

Jack watched as Keri mingled through the crowd, chatting with his family and some mutual friends. " . . .

only when I bend down like this." Mrs. Bastian demonstrated the move.

"Make an appointment with me for Monday morning, Mrs. Bastian. I will give you a thorough checkup then." She nodded and rejoined the group she was visiting with before she cornered Jack.

"You are looking pretty mesmerized, my friend. Is that the ex?" Linc asked as he offered Jack another beer.

"Yes, that's her," he said, taking the bottle from Lincoln and guzzling the cold liquid.

"Seems like you might still have a thing for her?" Lincoln asked with a grin as he leaned against the back of one of the wooden lawn chairs.

Jack sighed. "Is it that obvious?"

"Pretty obvious, man. What's her story?"

"She has been with her asshole boyfriend for a long time. I don't think there is much of a second chance there for me. I pretty much blew it the first time around."

"I think it's pretty obvious she has some feelings for you too, Jack. If you want her back, I think you should go for it." Lincoln tossed his empty bottle in the recycle bin and went to find his wife.

Razor Drake's Wild Turn
in the Road

When Jack and Chance ended up stationed at the same place overseas all those years ago, it was both a blessing and a curse. For the family, there was some solace that the two were stationed together and would have each other to rely on in times of stress. But that could turn into a double-edged sword. What if something happened at that particular base? The odds for both of them to be at the wrong place at the wrong time went up. None of them could have imagined that what really happened would change the course of their lives forever. One horrible event changed them both as people, did significant damage to their relationship as brothers, and changed the dynamics of the Cooke family as a whole.

It was thought that both Chance and Jack were going to make the military a career and stay in until it was time to retire. Things didn't end up working out that way for Chance. Both he and Jack were stationed at Bagram Air Base. At the time, Chance had been in the Air Force for eighteen years and Jack for ten years as his start was delayed by attending medical school. Jack was assigned to the Heathe N. Craig Joint Theater Hospital as a surgeon, and Chance was with the 455th Expeditionary Unit as a combat rescue officer. The two brothers were close, just two years apart in age, and they had always gotten along well. Jack's closest friend, Douglas Kramer, was a member of Chance's team as well as another mutual friend of theirs, Rick "Razor" Drake. The four were pretty much inseparable when they weren't tied up with work.

It was a particularly hot July evening when the combat rescue team was called out to rescue some injured pilots who had gone down on a training mission. Chance, Razor, and Doug loaded up with the other members of the team and immediately deployed to the crash site. Jack and his team prepared for the incoming wounded. Little did they know, their services wouldn't be needed for several days. The rescue team made it to the crash site and successfully rescued the pilots. On their way back to base, the helicopter experienced mechanical issues and went down, killing one of Chance's team members and one of the injured pilots. The rest of the team, along with the other rescued pilot, were missing.

The three days that followed were chaotic. There was misinformation, and it wasn't clear where they were or if they were safe. Jack was beside himself with worry. Waverly and the rest of the Cooke family back stateside were in a panic, waiting desperately for news. The other three combat rescue teams were activated and were searching for their comrades. Even with all those active searches taking place, it wasn't until the group got quite close to the base on foot that they were finally spotted and brought in for medical treatment and debriefing. The story they told forever changed things for all involved.

As they were trying to make their way back to base, the group was ambushed by insurgents. They were pinned down and the details about what happened were conflicting, depending on which of the members of the group were telling the story. Somehow in the chaos, part of the group came under fire from the other members of the team and a friendly fire incident occurred. Douglas Kramer was killed in action and the shooter was Chance Cooke. Jack was distraught. While he was relieved that his brother was safe, he was deeply impacted by the death of his friend. The weeks that followed were strained. Jack and Chance were fighting, words were exchanged, and the start of the now almost fifteen-year rift between the two brothers began. Soon, Jack was reassigned to Aviano Air Base in Italy, and Chance was discharged from the Air Force. The rift caused ripples throughout the family. For years, Cord, Jack and Chance's father, tried to negotiate peace between his two sons. Jack couldn't get past the loss of his friend at the hands of his brother even though he knew it was an accident. Chance couldn't get past the guilt of having killed one of his own team. It still haunted him all these years later.

Jack had swallowed the anger, the grief. He had never really dealt with it, never really thought about it until he received a call a few days after his retirement party. "Jack, it's Razor." He hadn't heard from his old friend in many years.

"Razor, how are you?"

"I'm good, Jack. I'm good. How about yourself?"

"Good, thanks! To what do I owe the pleasure?"

"I am going to be in your neck of the woods tomorrow. I'd love to have lunch with you and Chance and have the opportunity to catch up." Jack cringed. The thought of lunch with his estranged brother wasn't his idea of a fun time. Plus, painful memories were sure to come up. Jack thought back to Waverly's comments about fixing the rift and figured this was as good a way as any to start.

"Sure. I can move some things around. What time?"

"How about noon?"

"Sounds good. Let's meet at The Tulip Diner. It's on Main Street."

"Okay, I'll find it."

"Did you need me to coordinate with Chance?"

"No, I will give him a call. I'll see you tomorrow, Jack."

Jack made a few calls to move some patient appointments to later in the day. He closed down the office and drove home on autopilot, lost in his thoughts and memories from times past. He was not looking forward to tomorrow.

Razor made arrangements with Chance and their reunion was set.

Jack waited nervously at the table for Chance and Razor to arrive. He was hoping that Razor would get there first so he didn't have to try to make small talk with Chance. Both men arrived at the same time and walked in together, so Jack was off the hook. The three caught up on jobs, families, and the people they served with for the first few minutes. They ordered and the waitress refreshed their drinks.

"So, I'm sure you are wondering why I showed up in your tiny town out of the blue," Razor said, looking very serious. Jack and Chance nodded but did not speak. "A few months ago, I was diagnosed with an aggressive, inoperable brain tumor." Razor paused.

"Razor, I'm so sorry. Have you gotten a second opinion?" Jack asked.

"And a third. They all concur that my time here is short."

"That's tough, Razor. I'm sorry," Chance said, shaking his head in disbelief.

"So, that's part of why I am here. There is something I need to talk to both of you about. Something I have been carrying around for a long time."

Jack swallowed hard. He knew somehow that old wounds were about to be ripped open.

"All those years ago, when Doug was killed . . . " Razor's voice trailed off, full of emotion. Chance drew in a sharp breath, not wanting to dive into this topic either.

"Razor, it's ancient history," Chance said.

"Please, Chance, this is important. I need to get this off my chest. It wasn't you," Razor said.

"What do you mean, Razor?" Jack asked.

"It wasn't Chance that shot Doug. It was me," Razor was barely able to choke out the words. Jack and Chance were both stunned, silent, trying to process what they had just heard. "I am so sorry, Chance. When it came out that it was you who fired the shot, I thought I was in the clear. I wasn't man enough to speak up. I have carried that guilt around for all this time. Not only did I kill my friend, but I let you take the fall. I let you and Jack fight for all these years. I had to set the record straight before my time is up." Tears rolled down Razor Drake's cheeks. A wave of nausea washed over Jack as he tried hard to keep himself together. The waitress brought their meals. The three men sat in silence, none of them having any desire to eat their lunch.

Chance felt a combined fury and relief. "Do you realize what you've done? What you did to me? You ruined my military career, destroyed my life, Razor. My wife, my kids, my family, they all had to deal with this. I have spent the last fifteen years thinking I killed one of my best friends. My brother has hated my guts for the last fifteen years based on a lie." He spat the words, the anger evident in his voice. "How could you do this?"

"Chance, I'm so sorry." Chance stood and stormed out of the diner. Jack asked the waitress for the bill. "Jack, please say something."

"I'm not sure what to say, Razor. I think Chance is going to need some time to process this. I know I am." Jack paid the bill and stood to leave. "You take care of yourself," he said as he picked up his jacket and walked out the door.

Jack stopped by his office to call the two patients that were scheduled to come in that afternoon and rescheduled them for the following day. He couldn't concentrate. He drove home, found a beer in the fridge, and flopped down on the sofa in his living room. His mind was spinning. All those years of anger at Chance for nothing. The regret made him feel sick to his stomach again. He picked up his phone and dialed.

"Hello?"

"Hi there," he said.

"Jack, what's wrong?" Keri knew immediately that something wasn't right.

"Can you meet me for a drink? I can come to you."

"Uh, sure, I guess. What time and where?"

"Five o'clock? At the bar in the Marriott across from your office?"

"Sure. I'll see you then. Jack, are you sure you're okay?"

"I'll see you at five." Jack hung up, found his keys, and took off for Barber. He would be hours early but he didn't care; he couldn't stand to sit alone in his house. Picking up his phone, he thought about calling his brother Drew but decided against it. Then he thought about calling Linc, but he wasn't ready to share everything with him, so he decided to wait.

Once he arrived in Barber, he parked in front of the hotel. After paying the desk clerk for a room, he took the elevator to the fourth floor and found his room number. It was a struggle to get the key reader to work to unlock the door. Inside, he flipped on the TV and closed the curtains, flopping down on the bed with a sigh. Picking up the remote, he then mindlessly flipped through the channels. He was restless, antsy. After watching the news, the sports scores, a bad infomercial, and some disturbing daytime talk shows, Jack decided to take a shower. He stood under the stream of hot steamy water, wondering what was going to happen next. Surely, Chance would never want to speak to him or see him again. Jack had no idea what he would say to him even if he did have the opportunity. *How do you apologize for something like that?* He turned off the water, dried off, dressed, and went downstairs to wait.

Keri walked into the bar at about five minutes after five. It was almost empty, so finding Jack was easy. He was tucked away in a booth in the back corner. He stood as she approached the table. "You look beautiful," he said as he kissed her cheek. She had on black slacks and a coral shell, her curly shoulder-length light brown hair pulled up in a messy bun.

"Thank you, Jack. Now, are you going to tell me what's going on?"

"Let's order first." They motioned for the waitress and ordered their drinks. Jack sighed, unsure of where to begin. Keri had been kept in the loop on things related to Jack over the years as she and Waverly, Angelica, and Bits had remained close friends even after the divorce.

"I had lunch today with Chance and Razor Drake."

"I don't know who that is."

"He was on Chance's combat rescue team. We were friends back then." Keri nodded her head. "He came to tell us he was dying of an inoperable brain tumor."

"Oh, Jack! That's awful! I'm so sorry. Is that what has you so upset?"

"No, what has me upset is that he came to tell us that what we thought happened fifteen years ago wasn't what really happened at all, that everything I thought was a lie." Jack ran the fingers of his right hand through his hair in a quick deliberate motion, a telltale sign that he was frustrated or upset.

"I don't understand, Jack." Music from a live band erupted from the stage. "Is there somewhere quiet we can go?"

Jack nodded, leaving cash on the table to cover their drinks and a tip. He stood and took her hand, leading her through the lobby and to the elevator. They rode to the fourth floor, each lost in their own thoughts. He led her down the corridor to the room, unlocking the door without issue this time.

Keri took off her heels and curled up at the end of the small loveseat. "Tell me what that means, Jack. Everything was a lie?" Jack sank into the chair next to the loveseat.

"All this time I blamed Chance for Doug's death. I was so furious at him for killing my best friend. I thought he was cocky and careless and that Doug paid the ultimate price for that behavior and I couldn't forgive him." Jack's eyes welled up with tears. "And now, Razor Drake comes into town and informs us that he is the one who shot Doug, not Chance. That I spent all that time hating my brother for no reason. That Chance spent all those years carrying that burden for no reason. He left the Air Force because of this, Keri. He had to go to rehab to stop drinking because of what he thought he had done and because of how I treated him. All of it was because of a goddamned lie."

Tears were rolling down his cheeks. In all the time she had known Jack Cooke, almost forty years, she had never seen him display any kind of emotion. Even when he was angry, he was still even-keeled and reasonable. He never raised his voice and he most certainly didn't break the militaristic protocol of not crying set forth by his father. Keri reached for his hand. "How will he ever forgive me?" Sobs wracked his body. Keri stood and went to him, sitting in his lap and putting her arms tightly around his shoulders. He held her close, smelling her perfume, the familiarity of her touch still present after all the time that had passed.

"Jack, it wasn't like you accused him as he denied being the guilty party. He was the one who said things happened like they did. He believed the same thing." She tried to comfort him. Jack did not reply. "I think now is the time for you two to put this feud to rest and restart your relationship. It doesn't matter what the reason, only that both of you take advantage of the second chance."

His embrace tightened. Keri brushed the tears from his cheeks as he felt her soft lips against his. "Keri," he whispered her name, "I need you."

"I know, baby, I'm here."

Jack stood with Keri in his arms, carrying her to the bed. He laid down next to her, drawing her into his arms and kissing her. She pulled at his shirt in an effort to get it over his head. He obliged and then helped her remove her top and slacks. Jack smiled as he saw the coral bra and panties. Keri always loved lingerie and Jack always loved seeing her beautiful body as she modeled it. He undid his belt and took off his jeans and boxer shorts. Jack's muscular arms drew her in close, his hands caressing her shoulders and her back as he unclasped her bra. He slid his hands down her back to her hips, slipping her panties off and tossing them on the floor. He kissed her neck then kissed between her breasts as his hands gently explored her body. As he made love to her slowly with a tenderness she had forgotten, Keri realized just how much she still felt for him. "I love you," he whispered as he kissed her lips and then her neck. "I never stopped, not for one minute."

Keri did not respond. As her pleasure built, she was lost in the moment, remembering how happy they were together. Their issues were definitely not tied to the bedroom. Jack touched her, moved in ways that made her feel like he had made love to her just yesterday and not twenty years ago. He still knew all the right things to do to please her. A rush of pleasure overtook her, her fingers pressing into his muscular flesh as she clung to him.

"Jack . . . " she called to him. His arms tightened around her body, his breathing stilted as a series of pleasured moans escaped his lips. They laid together, relishing the physical gratification. "I should go, Jack," she said as she pulled away from his embrace.

"Please, don't go, Keri. Stay with me tonight." He tightened his embrace, not wanting to let her go. He kissed her softly.

"I can't, Jack. You know I can't."

"I want us to try again. I want us to be together. I love you, Keri."

"You don't even know me anymore, Jack. I've changed."

"Seems like we know each other pretty well still," he said with a sly grin.

Keri smiled as she got out of bed and put her clothes back on. Jack laid back against the pillows and watched her intently.

"Please don't go."

Keri piled her hair on top of her head in the same messy bun style it had been in when she arrived. She bent to kiss him, picked up her bag, and walked out of the hotel room.

Jack pondered the events of the day. He wondered where Chance was and how he was dealing with the news but didn't feel like he could call to find out. He got up from the bed, put on his boxer shorts, and picked up his cell phone. He dialed Linc.

"Hey, bud! What's shakin' in the giant metropolis of Collingswood, Kentucky, today?"

"Hey, Linc."

"Jack, what's up? What's going on?" Linc was instantly concerned.

"It's been quite a day here."

"What's happened?"

"What are the chances you and Clio could come up for a visit? I would love to see you and there is something I want to talk about in person." Jack heard a muffled conversation between Linc and Clio, not able to make out what they were saying, only that they were talking.

"We can leave first thing in the morning. We'll arrive around noon. Are you okay, Jack?"

"I will be. It will be good to see you both. Safe travels." He hung up his phone, dressed, checked out of the room, and drove home. While on his way back to Collingswood, his cell rang. It was Waverly. "How is he?" Jack asked.

"What does that mean, Jack? I was calling to see where he was. I haven't seen or heard from him all afternoon."

"Shit," Jack mumbled under his breath, worried. "Let me call you back." He hung up and dialed Drew.

"Hey, Jack."

"Have you heard from Chance?"

"I have. He's here with me."

"Thank God. How is he?"

"Pissed, relieved, rattled. About how you would expect him to be. How are you?"

"Not great, but I'll get through it. Can you stop by my place for a beer tomorrow afternoon? Linc and Clio will be here. I'd like to talk to you about what's happening, but I only have the energy to go through it once for both you and Linc."

"Sure. I'll wrap up early and head your way."

They said their goodbyes and hung up. Jack dialed Waverly.

"Jack . . . "

"He's fine. He is with Drew." Waverly let out a sigh of relief.

"What's going on, Jack?"

"You need to talk to Chance. You shouldn't hear about this from me. It's too important."

"You're scaring me, Jack."

"It's nothing like that, Waverly. Wait until he gets home from talking to Drew. He will fill you in."

The next morning, Jack dragged out of bed after a restless night. He was overwhelmed by guilt. There was such a sense of regret at the time lost with Chance. He was also feeling guilty about Keri. Guilt about what happened the previous day and that he put her in the position to cheat on Jagger, guilt about ever letting her go in the first place. He showered, dressed, and went to work. He saw the two patients that had appointments that morning then closed the office. He headed back to the house to wait for Linc and Clio to arrive. They pulled in the drive just before noon.

"You guys must have been up and out early," Jack said as he gave Clio a bear hug.

"Lincoln was worried about you, Jack. He wanted to get here as early as possible." He kissed her on the cheek. Lincoln got the bags from the trunk and the three went into the house. Linc set down the bags then he and Jack shared a manly embrace.

"You okay?" Linc asked. Jack nodded.

"I am. Drew is heading over in a bit for a beer. We can chat then. For now, let's go grab some lunch."

They drove to The Tulip Diner, found a table, and ordered their lunch. While they waited for their meals, they caught up on how things were going at the gallery.

"Her art is way more popular than my photos," Lincoln teased.

Clio laughed, shaking her head. "Don't believe a thing out of his mouth."

Jack smiled. Their happiness was evident. The reality of it was, the gallery was a smashing success, and they were considering opening locations in other cities. Clio filled Jack in on the latest with Mac and

Jae. Both were well, still with the fire department. They talked about Trey and how well things were going for him in London.

"How about Becks? Where is he these days?" Jack asked.

"He's still in the Middle East somewhere. You know he can't ever share what's happening. Last time we talked to him, he was pissed because they were going to embed that same journalist, Clementine Fisher, with his team again," Linc said, "Clio thinks he has a thing for her. I am not so sure." The waitress brought their lunch and they chatted as they ate, Jack filling them in on his brothers and his practice. They finished lunch and made the short drive back to Jack's farm.

The three sat outside on the screened porch, chatting. It wasn't long before Drew pulled up. Clio excused herself, saying she wanted to do some reading and maybe take a nap, giving the guys a chance to talk. The three men made small talk for a few minutes before Linc finally asked Jack to quit stalling and get down to business.

"So, there are two things I wanted to talk to you two about."

"Two things?" Drew asked. "I only knew about one. I might need more beer."

Jack explained the situation with Chance, starting at the very beginning since Linc had not been in the loop about any of the past history. His anguish was evident. Drew and Lincoln listened in silence as Jack spoke of the guilt, the regret, and the anxiety he was feeling about not knowing how to reach out or move forward. He paused, partly to hear if his friend or his brother had something to say, partly because he didn't know what else to tell them. He felt like he had bared his soul.

"You said two things," Drew reminded him. Jack sighed.

"I slept with Kari last night. I shouldn't have. I was emotional and feel like I pushed her into cheating on Jagger. I really can't stand him, but I am not that guy. I don't want to put her in that position."

"You weren't lying when you said that it had been quite a day yesterday," Linc said. "Drew, you talked to Chance yesterday. What's your take on where he is with all of this?"

"He's pretty overwhelmed, I think. He is very angry, a bit relieved, and he has the same kind of regrets, Jack. He feels like the lost time between you two was for nothing, that his career was ruined for no reason. He has always felt like doing what he is doing with the farm is a failure of sorts. His identity was so tied to leading the combat rescue team that in some ways he has been lost since leaving the military," Drew said.

"I had no idea," Jack said, shaking his head, "I have always wondered if it was the way I treated him, the things I said that contributed to him needing to go to rehab."

"Come on, Jack, don't be willing to take on all of Chance's burdens. He had problems with alcohol long before the falling out with you, long before the military." Drew tried to reassure him.

"So, Jack, what's your plan? How are you going to start to fix this rift with Chance?" Lincoln asked as he stood and gathered the empty bottles. He put them in the recycle bin and went to the kitchen to get refills, returning before Jack answered.

"I don't know, Linc. I am not even sure that if the situation was reversed that I would want to reconcile. I might feel like there was no fixing it."

"For what it's worth, I think he is open to putting this rift to bed once and for all. That was what he indicated when he was at my office yesterday," Drew said. "You two need to sit down and have a chat." Jack let out a sigh; thinking about that conversation made him incredibly anxious.

"And, let's not forget, we need a plan for the big reconciliation of you and Keri," Linc said with a grin.

"I'm not sure there is going to be any reconciliation. I want there to be, but I am not sure she feels the same way. I called her last night and she didn't answer. I texted her this morning and haven't heard anything back yet. She may try to work things out with Jagger or not tell him about last night at all."

The three men chatted the afternoon away. Clio stuck her head out of the sliding glass door to ask if Drew was staying for dinner. "No, thanks, Clio. I am going to go home and see Ange and Brax tonight. I was late last night." Clio finished up dinner as Drew left for home. Lincoln and Jack joined her at the dining room table.

"You didn't have to cook, Clio," Jack said as he sat down in front of a full plate.

"I didn't mind at all."

"So, Clio, I have a question for you."

"Sure, shoot."

"I need to have a difficult conversation with one of my brothers. I am dreading it and don't know how to start. Do you have any suggestions?"

"Well, why don't we invite all your family over for dinner on Sunday? Everyone can be here; and it will give you two the opportunity to chat without pressure. I can cook for all of us." Jack looked at Lincoln. Linc shrugged and smiled.

"It's as good a plan as any. You could invite Keri?" Linc suggested.

"We'll see about that. Are you sure, Clio? It's a lot of work," Jack said. Clio pulled out her phone and dialed her friend and partner in all things party related, Jae.

"Hey. You are off tomorrow, Sunday, and Monday. Right?" she asked when he answered.

"Yeah, I'm off. Why? What's up?"

"Get in the car and come to Jack's. We've got a dinner party to throw."

Jae laughed. "Well, okay then. I will get in the car first thing in the morning. Text me with a list of supplies or kitchen stuff you want me to bring."

"I will. Thanks, Jae. I'll see you tomorrow. Drive safely." She hung up her phone, turning her attention back to Jack. "See? Only half the work now."

Jack shook his head and smiled. They launched into conversations about what would be on the menu, indoor or outdoor dining, and other details. Jack sent a group text to all of his brothers and his parents. He was surprised when everyone accepted. The stage was set for a Sunday afternoon family dinner.

Early on Sunday morning, Clio pulled out her laptop and typed up menu cards. She and Jae had settled on the following:

Mixed green salad with balsamic vinaigrette
Creamy mushroom soup
Basil chicken with cream sauce
Prosciutto wrapped asparagus

Creamy risotto with butternut squash
Mango and strawberry cheesecake

She printed off twenty-one copies of the menu cards, ready to be put at the place settings when the tables arrived. Chance was dropping off tables, chairs, dishes, and linens he had borrowed from the distillery. Jack's out-of-town family had arrived yesterday. Since Linc, Clio, and Jae had taken the available beds at Jack's house, his parents were staying with Drew and Ange, and Owen and Gavin were staying with Jakob. She went into the kitchen to start her prep work while she waited for Jae to join her once he got up. She decided to tackle the chopping since there was a lot of it.

Jae joined her in the kitchen to find she had cut up the vegetables for the salad; the mushrooms, onions, and garlic for the soup; the tomatoes for the cream sauce; the asparagus; the butternut squash; and the fruit for dessert. She was now working on the pesto. "Wow! You have been busy! What time did you get up?" Jae asked her as he gave her shoulders an affectionate squeeze.

"I don't know, a couple of hours ago, I guess. I got in the chopping zone. I am going to finish up the pesto and wrap the asparagus. Could you whip up the cheesecakes and get them in the oven? They will need some time in the fridge before we serve them." Jae nodded and yawned as he poured himself a cup of coffee.

Linc wandered in to see how things were going. "Do you need my help, sweetheart?"

"When Chance gets here with the tables. We decided that since the weather will be nice, we can eat outside. If you could get the tables set up and the tablecloths on, that would be a huge help." Lincoln kissed her neck as he stood behind her, watching her stir the pesto.

"Consider it done."

The Past is the Future

The family arrived. It was the first time everyone had been together in one place in years. Jack had arranged the seating so that his father, Cord, was at one end of the massive table and his mother, Beverly, at the other.

Linc had talked Jack into inviting Keri. To his surprise, she had accepted.

Chance, Waverly, and their twin girls, Cassie and Kylie; Drew, Angelica, and their son Braxton; Jakob, and his now landlord Shiloh; Paxton and Elizabeth; Owen and Gavin; and the Charleston crew of Lincoln, Clio, and Jae were all in attendance.

There was visiting and mingling as everyone arrived while Jae and Clio finished up the last of the meal.

Lincoln let Jack know they were ready to start, and the two men worked the crowd to get everyone seated. Jack stood to make a toast. "Thank you all for coming. I am hoping this will be the first of many family get-togethers now that I am home. I've missed spending time with you all. I am also hopeful that this is the start of a new chapter for some of us." He looked at Keri and then at Chance. "A huge thank-you to my great friends Jae, Clio, and Linc."

The family raised their glasses and then ate the first course. Jae and Clio served and cleared course after course, letting everyone rest before dessert. The consensus was that the food was fantastic and everyone was stuffed. It was decided that they would chat for a bit while dessert was being laid out in the kitchen for folks to help themselves to whenever they were ready.

Lincoln went to the kitchen and insisted that both Clio and Jae leave the cleaning up to him. Waverly, Ange, Kari, Shiloh, and Bits backed him up, shooing the chefs out of the room and rolling up their sleeves to help. Kylie, Cassie, and Brax cleared the tables, pulled the linens, and put the tables and chairs in the back of Chance's truck.

Jack motioned to Chance, knowing he had put off the conversation for long enough. Jack grabbed two waters out of the cooler then he and Chance set off for a stroll and a chat. They walked in silence for a few minutes while Jack tried to gather his thoughts. "I don't really even know what to say to you, Chance. I'm sorry just seems so inadequate."

"You don't owe me an apology, Jack."

"I do. The things I said, the way I treated you for all these years, I don't know how to make up for that. I am sorry, Chance."

"Look, you were angry about Doug. I was angry at myself for all those years too, you know. We can't go back and change it, so I think we should just let bygones be bygones. Let's try to start from now and not waste any more time."

"When did you get to be so pragmatic?"

Chance smiled "I have a smart wife." "That you do, Chance."

"What's the scoop with you and Keri? You two getting back together?" Jack shrugged as he took a drink of his water.

"So, what now?" Jack asked.

"I don't know. We could have lunch this week." This time Jack smiled.

"Okay, but it's my treat."

"Deal."

The two men headed back to the rest of the family. Jack felt like a weight had been lifted from his shoulders. Things were finally heading in the right direction with Chance. Now he just had to figure out where things stood with Keri.

On his drive to work on Monday morning, Jack was curious about a group of people gathered in front of the movie theater. As he neared the end of the block, he discovered it was not in front of The Obsidian Theater but the storefront next door. There were balloons outside and a "Grand Opening" banner above the sign for Amaranth Apothecary. Jack didn't think much of it as he pulled into his parking spot behind his office.

Penniniah Graeber was opening her storefront and treatment rooms for her herbalist and acupuncture practice. Penniniah, who went by Penni for short, was an interesting character. She had been raised in an Amish community by very devout parents. Her three sisters and two brothers were still a part of the community, but Penni knew fairly early on that the Amish life was not for her. When she turned eighteen, she made the difficult decision to leave her family and pursue her own dreams.

She had always been interested in natural home remedies, so she worked odd jobs and took classes to become an herbalist. One of her instructors recognized her passion and how bright she was and invited her to study with him in China. Penni spent five years under his tutelage and had just returned to the states a few months prior, finding Collingswood, the storefront space, and an old farmhouse to rent. The location was just a couple of hours from the Amish homestead where she was born and her family still lived.

She missed her family but knew that there could never be any kind of reconciliation. Once she left the Amish community, all communication shut down. She was only thirty-two years old, the eldest of her siblings, so this saddened her. They had a lot of years left to be estranged. She often thought of them, wondering how they were and if they were happy.

Penni shook off the difficult memories and shifted her attention back to the grand opening. The space was a labor of love. The storefront was sleek and modern with the exception of the antique apothecary cabinets that lined the three walls, floor to ceiling. There was a railing that went around the room, suspended from the ceiling with an antique library ladder attached. When access to the higher drawers was necessary, she could move the ladder to where she needed. The antique wood gave the room an element of coziness and warmth.

In the back, there were two treatment rooms that had a spa-like quality of luxury and relaxation. The rooms were dimly lit with overstuffed furniture, soft music, and the smells of diffused oils. Her office, an homage to her time in China, and a large storage area completed the space. Her practice would be focused on mind, body, and spirit using traditional Chinese herbal medicine and acupuncture. Once clients were established, she would hire a massage therapist to provide her customers with another service to choose from.

Just a few days after opening, Penni had the unfortunate pleasure of meeting Dr. Jack Cooke. The encounter was unfortunate in that Jack was uncharacteristically angry about a couple of shared patients of theirs. Alice Peters, the local seamstress and laundress, had strained her back and gone to see

Jack, who prescribed some muscle relaxants. She came in for her follow-up appointment and gushed about how she hadn't needed to take even one of the pills he had prescribed for her because she had been to see Penni, and Penni had fixed her back using acupuncture.

Jack was furious, but he decided to let it go until a second patient, Henry Smith, the owner of The Tulip Diner, failed to fill his new prescription for cholesterol medication after having a conversation with Penniniah Graeber about supplements that he could try instead of going straight to prescription medications.

Jack stormed into Penni's store ready to do battle. "You are not a doctor, you know?" he spat the words across the counter at Penni.

"You must be Dr. Cooke," she said calmly. "I'm Penniniah Graeber. It's nice to meet you."

"Where do you get off telling my patients not to take medications I have prescribed for them?"

"I never told your patient not to take his medications. I just informed him of the alternatives he could try before he started down the path of medication."

"You know nothing about his patient history or if he is on any other medications or if the voodoo crap you 'prescribed,'" Jack used his hands to gesture air quotes, "is going to interact. You are dangerous." Penni took in a deep breath. It wasn't the first time she had dealt with skepticism.

"Just so you know, I took a full patient history on Henry. I assume that's who has you so worked up. Would you like me to pull his chart for you?"

"No, I don't want to see his 'chart.'" Again he made the air quote gesture.

"Just because I don't have M.D. after my name doesn't mean that I haven't had years of training. Don't discredit me just because you don't understand or because you disagree with what I do." Penni's voice was calm but firm.

"Just stay away from my patients." Jack turned and stormed out as angrily as he had come in. Penni sighed as the door slammed behind him.

Drew stopped by Jack's office when he was out running errands for the horse farm that afternoon. "Hey, brother, how goes it?" he asked as he came into the lobby.

"Fine," Jack snapped, still angry over his confrontation earlier that morning.

"Whoa, what's eating you?" Drew was surprised. Jack rarely got riled up about anything.

"Have you met the newest Collingswood business owner?" Jack asked bitterly.

"No. Who?"

"Her name is Penniniah Graeber, and she is an 'herbalist.'" Again Jack gestured air quotes.

"Okay, so, what about her?"

"She is telling my patients not to take the medications I prescribed and that they should take her leaves and berries instead. She is dangerous and irresponsible." Drew tried to stifle a grin. "What?" Jack demanded.

"There is a lot of evidence to support holistic treatments and their efficacy, Jack. I'm not sure it's fair to call her dangerous just because her approach is different than yours." This further infuriated Jack.

"Just go, Drew. I don't want to talk about this." He turned and headed for his office.

"Jack . . . "

At home that evening, Jack was restless. He tried calling Keri, but she did not take his call. They hadn't spoken since the dinner party and Jack was frustrated. Added to that, he couldn't get Penniniah Graeber out of his mind. If Jack was being honest with himself, he would have to admit that she was very attractive. She had long wavy brunette hair and lovely green eyes. Her kind smile lit up her face. While Jack was still annoyed about her interference with Henry Smith, he was also feeling bad about losing his cool. His temperament was usually so even-keeled that his outburst was out of character. He sighed, thinking to himself that he needed to apologize to her, and he was not looking forward to it. He made himself a sandwich, showered, and went to bed, but sleep eluded him. He tossed and turned all night and finally gave up in the early morning, getting up, getting dressed, and heading out for a run.

As he was walking down his treelined lane after his run, his phone rang. "Hello?"

"Still pissed at me?" It was Drew, calling to check in after yesterday afternoon's abrupt end to their conversation.

"No, sorry about yesterday."

"No worries. She had you pretty riled up, Jack. That's not like you."

"I know. I'm not sure why it made me so angry. I need to stop by there today and apologize. She shouldn't be contradicting what patients are told by their physician, but I could have handled it better for sure."

"Want to grab lunch tomorrow?"

"Sure. I'll meet you at The Tulip Diner at 11:30?"

"Sounds good, Jack. See you tomorrow."

Jack showered, dressed for work, and made the short drive to his office. He pulled into his parking space as Shiloh was getting out of her car. "Morning, Shiloh!"

"Good morning, Jack."

Jack went inside, brewed a pot of coffee, and reviewed his schedule for the day. He had three patients coming in. He pulled their charts and did a quick review. He had a couple of hours before his first appointment and decided that the time was as good as any to go to the apothecary shop to apologize to Penniniah. He locked the door as he left and walked the couple of blocks to her store.

Penni was behind the counter making notes in a book when Jack entered. She looked up from her writings as she heard the door and took off her glasses.

"Good morning, Dr. Cooke," she said in the same calm tone she had used the day before.

"Good morning. And it's Jack, please." He walked towards the counter. The day before he was so angry that he hadn't paid any attention to the store. It was quite impressive with the hundreds of drawers full of different, herbs, teas, and other concoctions.

"Alright, then. Good morning, Jack." She smiled at him.

"We kind of got off on the wrong foot. I wanted to stop by and apologize for being so angry yesterday."

"Well, thank you for that. Apology accepted. I'm sorry that you felt like I interfered with your patient. That certainly was not my intent."

"Would you mind reviewing what you recommended to Henry with me? I would like to note it in his chart and do some research so I know how it might interact with any future treatment plans."

"I would be happy to. Can I make you a cup of tea while we chat?"

"Um, sure." Jack wasn't much of a tea drinker.

"What kind would you like?"

"I don't know much about tea. Surprise me." Penni smiled. She turned and picked up a stainless steel basket from a glass tea pot. Jack watched as she moved through the store, finding the drawer with the tea she was looking for. She put the loose leaves into the basket and walked back to the counter. She filled the pot with boiling water from the electric kettle.

"Let me pull Henry's file." Jack nodded and Penni went down the hallway to her office. Penni paused at her desk, taking a deep breath. She was feeling a bit rattled by Dr. Cooke. She was certain he was someone she was going to do battle with on an ongoing basis, so his apology caught her off guard. His charm and good looks were also impossible to ignore.

Penni was still nursing her wounds from a difficult breakup. While studying in China, she had had a four-year relationship with the son of her mentor. Zhou Xiang was a handsome bachelor and businessman who was intrigued by the American woman that his father had brought home to train. They became friends and then quickly became lovers as he swept the inexperienced Penni off her feet. The challenge came when Penni wanted to move the relationship to the next level while Zhou Xiang did not. He had no intention of a long-term commitment, and when his father introduced him to a young and beautiful Chinese woman, their relationship ended abruptly. It wasn't that Zhou Xiang was in love with the young woman, but she was a good match for him and the status of his family. Some of the old traditions were still prevalent in the more modern China of today.

She found the file for Henry Smith and went back to the shop to talk with Jack, stopping to pour two cups of the Friendship Tea that had been steeping. She handed a cup to Jack and gestured for him to sit at the small conference table tucked in one corner of the shop. She picked up the file and her own cup of tea then joined him. Jack took a sip of the fragrant tea.

"Wow! This is quite tasty. What's in here?"

"This is Friendship Tea. It's a mixture of Earl Grey tea, lemon, orange, cinnamon, clove, agave, and honey. I'm glad you like it."

Penni scooted her chair closer to Jack and opened her file, sliding it towards him so he could see what she was referring to. "I discussed a few options with Henry. The first is taking a supplement called red yeast rice. It's extracted from rice that has been fermented with a particular type of yeast. The resulting substance has many compounds that are believed to lower cholesterol. The main thing is the monacolin K, which is the same statin chemically as one of the medications you prescribed."

Jack was impressed. He could see from the paperwork in her file that she had taken an extensive medical history. He noticed on the form that she actually asked many questions that went above and beyond what he knew about his own patient. It was obvious that she knew what she was talking about regarding the chemical processes and reactions in the body with the supplement that she had recommended to Henry. "What else did you recommend?"

"We discussed some dietary changes. Given his line of work, sometimes eating a consistently healthy diet is a challenge. We discussed the benefits of olive oil, vegetables, garlic, nuts, that kind of thing." Jack couldn't argue with any of that. He had the same conversation with most of his patients. "We also talked about additional supplements that he could explore if he didn't get results with the red yeast rice. The list included fish oil, which can help with good cholesterol in the blood and help remove bad cholesterol in the arteries; CoQ10, which does many of the same things as the fish oil; and niacin, which can tackle high triglycerides. We also discussed the use of essential oils via a diffuser and the benefits of increasing his levels of exercise."

Jack sipped his tea, contemplating the fact that he was totally out of line the previous day. He would never admit that to Penni, but he knew. He jotted down some notes to put in Henry's chart. "Thank you for reviewing this with me."

"You're welcome, Jack. I am glad you came by."

Jack took the last sip of tea and stood to leave. "Have a nice rest of your day, Penni."

"Thank you. You too." Jack picked up his notes and went to the door, looking over his shoulder for one last glimpse of her as he left.

The next few days were frustrating for Jack. He realized that some of the same issues he and Keri had experienced during their marriage were still issues. Jack had willingly shouldered all the blame from the divorce, associating the failures of their relationship with his almost constant absence. Realistically though, there were other challenges. Keri was a very indecisive person. She was very much a people pleaser, and as a result, she was unwilling to make a decision that she felt might upset someone. Doing what would make Keri happy was never a part of her decision-making criteria. Additionally, she was a very poor communicator. Rather than having difficult conversations, she preferred to shut down and avoid resolving any issues.

Jack stopped at the office mailbox on his way in to find a small box tied with a bright green ribbon on top of the letter mail. He went into his office, setting down his bag and the envelopes and untied the ribbon. Inside was a bag of tea, a metal strainer, and a note that read: *Friendship Tea for my newest friend. Penni*

Jack smiled. Penniniah Graeber had been on his mind quite a bit lately. His phone rang, interrupting his thoughts. "Hello?"

"Hi," Keri said. Jack was surprised to hear from her. "Can you meet me for lunch?"

"Sure. What time and where?" Jack asked, confirming that his calendar was open until later in the afternoon.

"11:30 at The Tulip Diner?"

"Okay, I'll be there." Jack wondered what the lunch was about. Keri had been avoiding him and any sort of conversation about where things stood between them.

At 11:15, Jack left his office to walk the couple of blocks to The Tulip Diner. When he arrived, he found that Keri already had a table and was waiting for him. He bent to kiss her cheek as he pulled out his chair and sat. "Hi," he said.

"Hi. How are you?" Keri was visibly nervous.

"Good, thanks. And you?" The conversation felt awkward and forced.

"I'm fine, Jack." She fidgeted in her chair. The waitress came by, Jack ordered a club sandwich and Keri a salad. They sat for a moment in uncomfortable silence.

"What did you want to talk about, Keri?"

"I wanted . . . there's something I wanted to tell you."

Jack sighed. "Okay, what?"

"I'm leaving, Jack. I have accepted a position at the corporate office in Seattle. I leave in a few days."

Jack swallowed hard, taking in what she had said. "Jagger? Is he going with you?"

Keri shook her head no. "Jagger ended things when he found out about us. He moved out last week."

"So, you are just going to run without giving us a chance?"

"There is no us, Jack. Sleeping with you was a mistake. We have both changed so much. There is no second chance."

The muscles in Jack's jaw tensed as she spoke. "Tell me you don't have feelings for me, Keri."

"That's irrelevant, Jack. We aren't good together."

"Why can't you ever give into your feelings?" The waitress brought their food, and the two picked at their meals in silence.

After a few tense minutes, Jack motioned to the waitress for the check. "Did either of you want me to box up your food?" she asked, seeing the plates had hardly been touched.

"Thanks, Joan, not for me," Jack answered as he pulled out his wallet. Keri shook her head no as Joan took the plates away.

It was in front of The Tulip Diner that Jack and Keri said their goodbyes. It just happened to be the exact moment that Penni drove down Main Street in her green 1957 Chevy pickup truck. As she passed by and saw Jack interact with this woman with such intensity, watching as he kissed her and embraced her, Penni was surprised at how sad she felt. She had been thinking of Jack a lot over the last week. It had never crossed her mind that he was in a relationship with someone else.

Jack returned to his office. He still had an hour before his next patient. He picked up his cell phone and dialed Linc.

"What's happening, my friend?" Linc asked as he answered the call.

"So, I just had lunch with Keri."

"Oh yeah? Do tell . . . " Lincoln was confident that the two of them would reconcile. He wanted his friend to be happy.

"She's leaving, moving to Seattle. Jagger ended things with her when he found out about our night together. So now, instead of trying to work things out with me, she is going to run." Lincoln could hear the frustration in Jack's voice.

"I'm so sorry, Jack." Lincoln didn't know what else to say.

"Well, at least it's done. No more limbo. I can move on now, I guess."

"Do you want to come down for the weekend? Or, do you want us to come up?"

"I'm okay, Linc. But, talk to Clio. Let's get something on the calendar. I always love seeing you guys."

"I will, Jack. We will get together soon."

"I've got to run, I have a patient coming in."

"We'll talk soon." They disconnected the call, and Jack opened the chart for his incoming patient to read over his past history in preparation for his appointment.

A couple of blocks away, Penni Graeber was having a difficult time concentrating on her own work. Thankfully, she did not have patients coming in that afternoon, but the research she was working on was progressing slowly. She read and reread the same paragraph over and over with no retention of the words. She finally gave up, setting her printed pages aside, and got up to make a pot of tea. After her breakup with Zhou, she hadn't really thought about another relationship. But since Jack had come to her store to apologize almost two weeks ago, he had been occupying her thoughts and dreams, dreams like she had never had before.

A few days later, she ran in to Jack at Wagonner's while she was stocking up on groceries. "Hey Penni!" She turned to see his handsome face.

"Oh, hi, Jack." She was flustered, instantly nervous.

"How have you been?" he asked casually as he put a bag of potatoes in his cart.

"Good, thanks. How about you?"

"I'm good. How are things at the apothecary?"

Penni smiled. "Things are going well. I am thinking of hiring a massage therapist to add to the services I offer. How about things with you? There never seems to be a shortage of folks needing some sort of medical care."

It was Jack's turn to smile. "That's true. Work is going well." There was an uncomfortable silence between them for a few moments. "Penni, do you want to have a cup of tea with me sometime?"

"Well, I'm not sure your wife would like that much."

"What makes you think I have a wife?" Jack asked, surprised.

"Oh, I just assumed. I saw you with a woman in front of The Tulip Diner the other day."

Jack shook his head. "That was my ex-wife. She moved to Seattle this week. Definitely not my wife. I'm not seeing anyone." Penni couldn't decide if she heard a hint of bitterness in his voice or not. "So, what do you say? Tea at The Tulip Diner?"

"How about tea at my shop instead? I have a lot more choices. Tomorrow, after work?" Penni was feeling a flurry of emotions: fear, excitement, anxiety. She couldn't believe how relieved she was to find out that he wasn't in a relationship.

"That sounds great. How about 5:30?

"Perfect. I will see you then." Penni was glad the exchange was over. Jack Cooke had her completely riled up.

At home that evening, Jack found himself thinking about Penni Graeber. Even though things with Keri were still fresh, Jack couldn't help but think about what it might be like to be with Penni. She was about as different from Keri as she could be: confident, defiant, stubborn, unafraid. She was also smart and beautiful. Jack sighed as he changed positions, trying to get comfortable on the sofa to watch a movie. He drifted off into a restless sleep.

The next morning, Penni awoke before her alarm sounded. She laid in bed under the covers, thinking that it was too early for a fall chill. Her mind was racing with thoughts of Jack and their date for tea. After throwing back the covers, she slipped her bare feet into her fuzzy tan slippers. She yawned and stretched as she walked towards her closet.

Once the closet door was open, she assessed her choices, feeling like everything she had was drab and frumpy. Sighing, she turned towards the bathroom, leaving the decision on what to wear until after her shower. As the hot water pelted her back, she thought of Jack. He was charming and handsome. She let her mind wander, thinking of what it might be like to feel him kiss her. *What is wrong with me? He only wants to have tea.* Penni shook her head, bringing herself back to reality.

Finished with her shower, she dried off, put on some powder, lip gloss, and mascara then blew her hair dry, deciding to wear it down instead of pulled up in its usual chaotic bun. Back at her closet, she settled on chocolate-brown leggings, a soft orange cowlneck sweater, and a pair of chocolate riding boots. She made a piece of toast and a cup of tea then headed out the door to work, anxious to see Jack that evening.

Jack wasn't faring much better as he waited for the day to pass so he could see her. He hadn't slept much the night before, finding it difficult to get her out of his mind. Jack had gone for a long run before work then showered and dressed in dark jeans, a pale gray dress shirt, and a dark gray blazer. Thankfully, he had a busy day of patients that would keep his mind occupied. He chatted for a moment with Shiloh, who was having a cup of coffee in their shared space behind the building, and then went in to start his day. While pondering whether he should stop by The Perfect Petal later that afternoon to pick up some flowers for Penni, he realized that she didn't really seem like the flower type of girl. He picked up his phone and dialed his brother.

"Hey, do you have time to do me a favor today?" Jack asked Jakob.

"Sure. I don't have anything 'til this afternoon. What's up?"

"I am having tea after work today with Penni Graeber." Jakob smiled. "I wanted to take her some flowers or something, but she doesn't strike me as the flower type. I was hoping that you might have some ideas and that you could put together something for me?"

"I could put together a basket of herbs that are used to make tea if you like." It was Jack's turn to smile.

"I will leave it in your capable hands. Thank you for the help, Jakob."

"I'll drop something by your office after lunch."

After a quick internet search, Jakob headed to the garden center with a list of herbs. He chose lavender, lemon verbena, mint, thyme, chamomile, jasmine, rosemary, and lemon grass. A large pale green wicker basket caught his eye as he wandered the aisles of choices. He stopped at the counter where they assemble arrangements and wreaths and requested a large bow. The woman behind the counter presented him with several ribbon options. Jakob selected a pale green with yellow polka dots. He left her to tie the bow while he picked up soil and organic plant food. He picked up the bow and checked out before loading the items into the back of his truck.

On his way back to his apartment, Jakob decided to stop at The Age of Vintage, the local antique shop, to see if Pierre, the owner, had any old teacups that might match the basket.

Pierre went into the storage room having the perfect set in mind. He called out questions about how Jakob was and how his brothers and parents were doing while he looked. "Eureka!" he called out as he found what he was looking for. "What do you think of these?" He showed Jakob the set of two cups, two saucers, and a

---

cream and sugar set to match. They were creamy white with a pale green fern pattern and a gold rim.

"Those are perfect, Pierre," Jakob said. Pierre beamed. He loved finding just the right thing for someone. He wrapped the cups and saucers in gold tissue paper and put them in a fancy gold gift bag with The Age of Vintage logo then placed the cream and sugar set in a perfectly sized gold box. Pierre topped the box with a beautiful gold bow. "Thank you so much, Pierre."

"You are most welcome, my friend."

Jakob drove to the apartment and assembled the basket before heading to Jack's office to drop off the gifts. Jack smiled as Jakob came into his office with the magnificent basket.

"You outdid yourself, brother," he said as Jakob placed the basket on his desk.

"Wait, there is more in the truck." Jakob walked back to the truck to retrieve the box and the bag. "I picked these up at Pierre's. I'm not sure if you will think it's too much." Jack carefully unwrapped one of the cups and saucers from the bag. "There are two of each." Jack opened the box and looked at the cream and sugar set. He was quiet for a moment.

"They are perfect and so thoughtful. Thank you, Jakob."

"No problem. Happy to do it. Shiloh and I are going to check out the Fall Fest on Friday. Maybe you two should join us," Jakob suggested as he stood to leave.

"Maybe we will." The brothers shared a manly embrace as Jakob left.

Penni spent the day trying to stay busy. She had a few appointments and walk-in customers. The rest of the time was spent researching some new treatments. At last it was 4:45, the time that Penni had planned to close the shop, freshen up, and start the tea.

She went into the bathroom to brush her hair and freshen her makeup. As she walked by the counter in the main storefront, she flipped on the electric kettle then walked to the cabinet and drawer containing the tea she had selected. Penni filled the metal basket with Apricot Amaretto tea, put it in her white ceramic teapot, and then poured the steaming hot water from the kettle. She placed the lid on the pot and picked up the remote to turn on some soft music.

Jack loaded the gifts into the back of his truck and drove the few blocks to Penni's store. Once he found a place to park, he got out, put on his jacket, and picked up the basket in one hand. Tucking the box under his arm and holding the gift bag in the other hand, he walked to Penni's store. Juggling his packages, Jack opened the door. The storefront was empty, the lights were low, soft music was playing in the background, and the faint scent of almonds and spices filled the air.

Jack set the basket and the packages on the table then browsed the labels on the apothecary cabinet drawers. There were items he had never heard of in some.

Penni came in carrying a large tray filled with plates of cheeses and crackers, small sandwiches, and fruit and vegetables with dip.

"Hi, Jack," she said as she set the tray on the counter. Jack turned and walked towards her, thinking to himself how beautiful she looked.

"Hi there," he said as he gently embraced her. "You smell fantastic," he said softly as he took in her scent. Penni smiled.

"Thank you."

"I brought you something."

"You did? Jack, you didn't need to do that."

He smiled. "I hope you like it." Jack motioned towards the table. Penni saw the basket and gasped.

"Oh, Jack! It's beautiful!"

"I was going to bring you flowers, but I hope you like this better." Penni nodded and smiled. "Here, open your packages." Penni's hands were shaking as she pulled one of the teacups out of the bag and removed the gold tissue paper.

"Jack!" she exclaimed as she inspected the delicate china.

"Do you like it?"

"I love it! They are so beautiful. Thank you so much! What a lovely gift." Penni was gushing.

"All the credit goes to my brother, Jakob. He owns his own landscaping business, so he picked out the plants and the china as well."

"I might need to call him. I desperately need some foliage around here."
"He can definitely take care of you. I will give you his number before I leave." Penni finished unwrapping the china and carried it to the sink, giving it a quick wash and rinse so she could use it to serve the tea. Jack set the basket aside and cleared the wrappings from the table. Penni returned with all the tea accoutrements on a tray and placed it in the center of the table. She

brought over the plates of food and motioned for Jack to sit down.

There was an uncomfortable lull in the conversation as Penni poured the tea. "Cream and sugar?" she asked.

"I don't know. I don't know a thing about tea. What should I add?"

Penni smiled. She put a bit of sugar and a dash of cream in his cup and gave it a stir. "Try that."

Jack took a sip of the hot liquid.

"Wow. Penni, that is delicious. What is it?"

"It's called Apricot Amaretto. It has black and green tea, marigold flowers, almonds, honeybush, and apricot."

"What's honeybush?"

"Oh. It's a plant found on the cape of South Africa. It's also called Cyclopia and has lots of health benefits like boosting the metabolism, treating asthma, and soothing a sore throat. It's also full of antioxidants. Good stuff!"

Jack smiled. "I always learn something when we get together." He popped a grape into his mouth and took another drink of tea. They chatted while nibbling at the snacks.

"Do you want to switch from tea to wine?" Penni asked. "I can open a bottle of white or red. You choose."

"Red would be great." Penni went to her office and pulled a bottle from the cabinet, returning with a corkscrew.

"Here, let me." Jack took the bottle and opened the cork. Penni got two wine glasses and Jack poured.

"Let's move somewhere more comfortable," she suggested as she carried her glass to the large overstuffed sofa. Jack followed with his glass and the bottle.

"So, you mentioned your brother earlier. Is it just the two of you?"

Jack laughed. "You must be new here. No, I have six brothers. No sisters but some great sisters-in-law. Most of us live here in town or at least close by. What about you?"

"I have three sisters and two brothers, but I haven't seen them for a very long time."

Jack paused, pondering what she had said. "Can I ask why?"

Penni smiled, thinking his voice was soft and kind. "Sure. I was born into an Amish community a couple of hours from here. I decided that the lifestyle was not for me, so I left when I turned eighteen. As is customary when someone leaves, there is no further contact. I haven't seen my siblings or my parents since then. That was fourteen years ago."

Again, Jack paused. "I find everything about you fascinating, Penni. I knew from our first meeting that you were a strong woman, but I had no idea how strong until now."

Penni took a sip of her wine. "Will you tell me about your brothers and your parents? I would love to hear about them."

"Sure. My parents, Cord and Beverly Cooke, live just outside Chicago. My father was a lifelong military man in the Air Force and my mother was the patient soul who tried to raise seven completely rowdy and obnoxious boys."

Penni smiled as she watched him describe his family. The fondness was evident.

"My oldest brother, Chance, lives close by. He has a large farm and grows corn for the distillery. He has been married forever to Waverly, and they have two girls that are getting ready to graduate from high school. Then there is my brother Paxton. He also lives close by. He is a builder and works for Timberline Construction. He has been married to Bits forever. They don't have any kids."

"Bits?" Penni asked with a grin. Jack chuckled.

"Elizabeth. We have all known each other since we were kids. Her nickname stuck I guess. Then there is me—I am the third in line. Next is my brother Gavin. He is single, an architect, and lives in Chicago. Then Drew lives here with his wife Angelica, who we call Ange and their twenty-year-old son, Braxton. Drew manages the Silver Sage Thoroughbred Horse Farm in town. Then there is Jakob. He is single, but I am guessing not for long. He is the one I was telling you about with the landscaping company. And last, the baby of the family, my brother Owen. He is a college professor at the University of Illinois in Chicago."

"It sounds like a lovely family. Are you close to them?"

"It's getting better. I was in the military myself. I just retired a few months ago, so I have been stationed all over the place and didn't really have an opportunity to spend much time with them. We are working on reconnecting."

"That's so great, Jack. I am envious that you have the opportunity to get to know them again but so happy for you as well."

"There is no chance for you to reconcile with your family?" Penni shook her head no, her expression one of sadness. Jack reached for her hand. "I'm sorry, Penni," he said softly.

"It is what it is, I guess." Jack smiled as he ran his thumb gently over the back of her hand.

"So, you were married?" Penni decided to be forward.

"I was, but it was a long time ago. How about you? Have you ever been married?"

"No. I was seeing someone when I lived in China, but that ended. I haven't really dated anyone since."

"Why not?" Jack asked.

"I guess because I don't want to open myself up for that kind of hurt again."

"I can understand that. I haven't really dated anyone seriously since my divorce which was two decades ago. I thought maybe things would be different between the two of us when I came back here. But, they weren't. All the same issues we had before were still issues."

"Do you still love her?"

"I care about her certainly, but I am not in love with her. What about things with your ex? Are you still in touch?"

"No, things ended badly. We are not in touch and I don't anticipate us ever being in contact."

They continued chatting about her time in China and Jack's travels with the military as they finished off the bottle of wine.

"It's late, Penni. We should call it a night," Jack said reluctantly. "Can I drive you home?"

"That would be nice, actually. I think I had a bit too much wine."

"Let me help you clean up."

"Leave it, I will get it in the morning. Let me get my bag." Penni went to her office to retrieve her purse. As she returned to the storefront, she dug in her bag for her keys. Jack held the door for her and then waited for her to lock up. He helped her into his truck and got in on the driver's side.

"Where to?" he asked.

"I am renting the old Kellogg place. Do you know where that is?"

"I haven't been out that way in years," Jack said as he pulled on to Main Street. There was no traffic that late in their small town. "I had a really nice time with you tonight, Penni."

She smiled. "I had a really nice time too, Jack."

"You know, my brother and his girlfriend, or soon-to-be girlfriend, or whatever are going to the Fall Fest in Barber on Friday night. He invited us to join them. I would love it if you would go with me."

"I would love to! Thank you for the invitation."

They rode in silence for a few minutes. Jack turned into the long curvy driveway leading to the large old farmhouse.

"It's a great old house," Jack said.

"I love it here. I am hoping one day the Kelloggs will sell it to me." Jack parked and turned off the truck.

"Let me walk you to the door."

"That's not necessary, Jack."

"Let me walk you to the door, Penni." He got out of the truck and went around to open the passenger side door, offering Penni his hand to help her out of the truck. They walked together up the front path to the large wraparound porch. Penni dug in her bag for her keys and unlocked the front door.

"Do you want to come in?"

"I shouldn't, although I hate for the evening to end. I should go, but I will pick you up in the morning around 8:30."

"You don't need to do that, Jack."

"Oh, no? And how exactly are you planning on getting to work in the morning?" Jack gave her a sly grin.

"Well, I hadn't really thought about it."

"So, I will pick you up at 8:30. We will stop at The Tulip Diner for breakfast and I will drop you at your shop."

Penni smiled. "That sounds great. Thank you, Jack, for the lovely gifts and an even lovelier evening." Jack stepped towards her, his arms gently encircling her waist.

"Thank you, Penni. I will see you in the morning." He softly kissed her forehead, turned, and walked back to his truck.

Penni unlocked the door and went in, closing it behind her, leaning heavily against the old oak door. She sighed, thinking about how good it felt to be in his arms. She was unsure what she wanted, what Jack wanted. But she wanted to see where things went.

Jack was lost in his own thoughts on his drive back to his farm. He was totally mesmerized by Penniniah Graeber. She was different from any other woman he had ever met. He was looking forward to seeing her in the morning.

"You look beautiful," Jack told her as she locked her front door. Her hair was braided down her back. The greenish-gray frames of her glasses matched her sweater. Her black skirt met her black boots mid-calf.

"Thank you, Jack." He opened the door of his truck and helped her inside.

"What does your day look like?" Jack asked.

"I have a couple of acupuncture patients later this morning and a consultation with a woman from Barber this afternoon. She wants to talk about things she could take to help her menopause symptoms. Then I have to finish my research and write an article for *The Herbalist*. It is due on Friday. What about you?"

"I have a few patients today, run-of-the-mill stuff mostly. One of these days, you will have to teach me something about acupuncture. I have no idea how it works."

"Sure! I would love to tell you about it."

"What is your article about?"

"A genus of plants in South Africa that shows very promising results in slowing the symptoms of Parkinson's."

"Can I read it?"

"Um . . . sure, I guess. When it's done." Jack found a place to park in front of The Tulip Diner. They went in and found a table for two.

"Good morning, Dr. Cooke."
"Good morning, Joan. This is Penni Graeber. She owns the apothecary store down

the street. Penni, this is Joan Carter."

"It's nice to meet you, Joan."

"Nice to meet you too. What can I get for you two?"

"I'll have my usual," Jack said.

"And for you?"

"I will have the fruit and yogurt, please, and a cup of hot tea," Penni said. Jack and Penni chatted while they waited for their food. Joan brought them their meals.

"So, tell me more about this article you are writing," Jack said.

"There are about seventy-five extracts that have been discovered in this genus of plants, and they are currently testing them in the treatment of Parkinson's with some remarkable outcomes. The article is about what they know so far, what results they have seen, and what the next steps are to advance the extracts into the marketplace."

"Interesting. Is there a regulating body that approves holistic treatments?"

"In some cases, the FDA. It's actually quite complicated."

"I can imagine." They finished their breakfast and Jack paid the check.

"Let me walk you to your shop."

"That's really not necessary, Jack. I can make it two blocks all by myself."

"Oh, believe me, I know. I just like your company, so I'd like to walk you to your shop. Are you okay with that?" Penni smiled and nodded. They strolled the two blocks with no words exchanged. "Do you want me to come in and help you clean up?" Jack asked when they got to her door.

"Thank you, Jack, but no. You go ahead and get started with your workday."

"I will pick you up around six tomorrow night. Do you want me to get you here or from your house?"

"Pick me up here. It's closer. I'm looking forward to tomorrow night!"

"Me too. I'll see you then." He kissed her cheek as he turned and walked back up the block towards the diner to retrieve his truck.

Thursday was a busy day for both Jack and Penni, full of patients and operational tasks to complete. Midday, Penni was surprised by a delivery of a beautiful bouquet of purple lilacs tied with a deep purple bow. The card read:

Just in case you are that flower kind of girl after all. If anyone would know the meaning of these flowers, it would be you.

I will see you tomorrow night.

Jack

She did know the meaning: lilacs symbolized the first emotions of love. Her heart was pounding. Penni picked up her phone and dialed Jack's number.

"Hello?"

"They are beautiful, Jack. Thank you so much."

Jack smiled. "You're welcome. I am glad you like them."

"How's your day going?"

"Good, nothing exciting. What about you? How is your article coming?"

"It's good, almost finished I think. I will give it the once over tonight and again in the morning before I push the button to submit."

"Hey, Pen, gotta run, my next patient just arrived."

"Thank you again for the flowers, Jack. I'll see you tomorrow."

Penni unlocked her front door as her phone chimed letting her know she had a text message:

Jack: *I am having dinner with my brother and his family tonight, but I wanted you to know I am thinking about you and looking forward to seeing you tomorrow evening.*

Penni: *You are very sweet, Jack. I am looking forward to tomorrow as well. Have fun with your family tonight.'*

Penni couldn't wipe the smile from her face as she made a sandwich for dinner and sat down to put the finishing touches on her article before she submitted it the following day. She found it difficult to concentrate, her thoughts drifting to Jack over and over.

After what felt like an agonizingly long day for both Penni and Jack, it was finally time to meet. Jack drove the short distance to Penni's shop. As he entered the shop, he breathed in the sweet woody scent. It was subtle but warm and inviting.

"Hi there," she said as she came into the storefront from the hallway.

"Hi yourself," he said as she walked towards him. He put his arms around her. "Would it be too forward to tell you that I missed you?"

Penni smiled and returned his embrace. "I missed you too, Jack."

"Are you ready to go?"

"I am. Let me grab my bag and a sweater."

They chatted about a variety of things on the drive to Barber, including her article.

"I was doing some poking around. *The Herbalist* is a pretty big publication, Penni. It's really impressive that you are being published by them."

"Thank you. I sent off my article today. It should be published online and in the next issue of their print media."

"I can't wait to read it." Jack parked the truck in the dirt lot designated for the Fall Fest. "I haven't been to this in years. It's been a fall staple around here since I was a kid."

They stood in line, paid the entrance fee, and then went through the arch of grapevines and fall leaves to enter the festival. Held on a large empty lot, it was set up like a fair. There were booths lining the aisles filled with vendors selling crafts and food with rides and games intermixed. In the back corner of the property was a huge corn maze. There were artists doing caricatures, pumpkin carving stations, photo booths. It was really quite elaborate.

"This is impressive!" Penni was marveling at the variety of sights and smells. Jack's cell phone rang.

"Hey, where are you?" he asked his brother. "Okay, we will meet you there." Jack took Penni's hand and led her toward the corn maze where they found Jakob and Shiloh. Introductions were made and the four set off to explore the festival. Shiloh and Penni chatted as Jack and Jakob walked a few steps ahead.

"So, what's the scoop with you two?" Jakob asked.

"I could ask you the same thing." Jack retorted.

"Fair enough."

The group stopped to browse at several booths. Jakob and Penni did an inventory of the fall plant booth put on by a local garden center and talked about what kind of foliage Jakob could put together for her shop. As they were strolling down one of the aisles, Shiloh noticed a huge stuffed pig that looked a lot like her pet pig, Presley. She pointed it out to the group and Jakob and Jack set out to win the game by shooting the target with the air rifle. Jack tried his hand a couple of times, failing miserably and taking a ribbing from the group. Jakob tried as well, not faring much better. The two brothers looked at each other and at the same time said, "We need Chance." Chance was an exceptional shot because of his military training. Jack pulled out his cell phone.

"Jack, before you call, let me give it a go," Penni said. Jack and Jakob looked at each other, grinning.

"Okay, sure." Jack gave the vendor three tickets. Penni picked up the air rifle and easily cleared the target. Both brothers were shocked. The vendor asked Penni which prize she wanted and she claimed the pig, handing it to Shiloh.

"Thank you so much, Penni!"

"You're welcome!" Penni said with a huge grin.

"You better be on your best behavior, Jack!" Jakob joked.

"No kidding! How did you learn to shoot like that?"

"We hunted when I was a child. I've been shooting a gun since I was a little girl."

"Every time we're together, Penni, you never cease to amaze me."

The foursome wandered around the festival, chatting and laughing. They stopped for a bowl of butternut squash soup and a cup of hot apple cider then continued to make their rounds. Penni was introduced to Jack's niece, Kylie, who was covering the Discovery Gallery Arts Center booth with Devina McLaine, the owner. Kylie worked there part-time helping with displays and events. She also got to meet Chance, who was there with the Aegis Distillery team.

Around 10:30, the weather took a turn for the worse. Rain pelted them and the air grew very chilly. Penni pulled her sweater out of her bag and Jack put on his sweatshirt. Jakob, Shiloh, Jack, and Penni hurried to the parking lot, said their goodbyes, and left for home. As they drove the almost thirty-mile distance between the two towns, the temperatures plummeted and the rain turned to ice. For the first time since the early 1960s, the temperature dropped almost fifty degrees in just a couple of hours. The roads were treacherous as they crawled back to Collingswood. Jack's cell phone rang. Wanting to concentrate on the road, he handed it to Penni. "Dr. Cooke's line," she answered. It was Shiloh calling from Jakob's phone.

"We just wanted to see if you were okay. We must have taken a different route."

"We are on 74."

"Okay, we took 441. Have Jack call Jakob when he gets home."

"Okay, you guys be careful."

"You too!" They disconnected as Jack slowed even more. The windshield wipers and defroster were having a difficult time keeping up with the freezing rain now coating everything in its path.

"Pen, can you find Chance's number in my cell and call him? I want to see if he and Kylie are together." Penni found the number and dialed, putting the phone on speaker.

"Hey, have you left yet?" Jack asked as Chance answered.

"Yeah, I am on 441. Where are you?"

"We are on 74. It's awful."
"Pretty awful this way as well."

"Jakob and Shiloh went that way too. What about Kylie? Is she with you?"

"No, she was riding home with Rowan and Brax. If I would have known it was going to get this bad, I would have made them ride with me."

"I'm sure they will be fine. I am going to drop Penni off at her place and head home. I will check in later. Drive safe." They disconnected. Penni and Jack were both quiet, tense due to the deteriorating conditions. He turned into her driveway and helped her from the truck to the porch. "Do you have any salt or sand? These steps are dangerous."

"I can put down some salt, Jack. You should go before it gets any worse." Jack nodded. "Be careful." He kissed her softly on the cheek.

"I'll call you in the morning and let you know what time I will be by to pick you up and take you to your car."

"Thank you for tonight, Jack. I had a wonderful time."

Jack got in the truck and waited for the wipers to break through the icy film on his windshield. Relieved, Jack pulled into his driveway. He was glad to be off the roads. He carefully walked across the slick driveway to his door and into the house, turned on the lights, and put on a pot of coffee. He wouldn't have time to enjoy a cup though as a knock at his door would change everything. It was Jakob . . .

PAXTON

A Crisis in Confidence

Paxton took a long swig from his beer bottle and surveyed the crowd in Jack's back yard. He couldn't shake the feeling of restlessness he had been carrying around for several weeks. He watched as his brothers mingled with family and friends. He watched his wife of almost thirty years as she laughed with her sisters-in-law about something Jack had said. Why was he so unsettled? He had a good life with a wife he loved, a good job that he enjoyed, a raucous family that could work his nerves, but they were also his favorite people.

He felt unsettled, bored, unsatisfied; none of those words adequately described it though. The right words to describe what he was feeling somehow remained out of his reach. He and Elizabeth (Bits) had been fighting. They were fighting over stupid things, and he knew that she was worried about him and how things were going between them. What he didn't know was that his wife had confided in his brother, Gavin, about the issues they were having. Pax was a private person and would not like the fact that she had shared their problems, especially with one of his brothers. Gavin and Bits were close friends. They were the same age and had known each other since they were children.

Pax's thoughts drifted to Potter Wendell. He had seen her for the first time in years a few days prior at The Tulip Diner. Potter and Pax had dated in high school and most thought that she was going to end up becoming his wife. Potter had broken Paxton's heart when she ran off with Digger Williams. The two of them suddenly eloped, leaving Pax devastated. He had turned to Elizabeth for comfort and they ended up getting married shortly after.

While his family loved Bits, they had cautioned him against marrying her as they felt it was a rebound relationship. Their union had turned out to be a solid one though. They were happy together, had decided not to have children, and their life together was good. But ever since seeing Potter, Paxton had felt even more unsettled. He was thinking of what might have been. Potter was now divorced from Digger and was back in town for good, working for Sibrina Banyon at Dream Home Realty.

"So, have you seen her?" Chance asked.

"Potter? Yeah, I saw her. Why do you ask?"

"Oh, come on, Pax. That had to be strange."

"It was no big deal." Pax lied to his brother. He couldn't get her out of his mind. He couldn't stop thinking about the past and what his life might have been like with her. Would he have a different life, a different job, children? He couldn't help but yearn for the time when the two of them were together. First love is difficult to shake when it rears up in your face even after many years.

"What's happening over here?" Drew asked as he joined them.

"I was just listening to Pax lie about it being no big deal that Potter Wendell is back in town," Chance said.

"Wow. When did that happen? Is she visiting or did she move back?"

"I saw her a few days ago. I don't know how long she's been back, but she is back. She is divorcing. I think she is working for Sibrina," Pax explained.

"Does Bits know she's back?" Drew asked.

"I don't know. I haven't told her. It's not really a conversation I want to have. She isn't going to be thrilled."

"She's going to find out. Waverly saw Potter at Waggoner's yesterday. I'm pretty sure it's going to come up. If not today then soon," Chance said.

"Great," Pax muttered. He sighed as he walked towards the cooler in search of another beer.

Paxton was wading through expense reports on one of his many projects when his cell phone rang. "Paxton Cooke."

"Hi, Pax."

"Potter. Hi."

"How are you?"

"Good, thanks, and you?"

"I am good. Thanks for asking."
"What can I do for you, Potter?"

"Meet me for a drink? I would love for us to properly catch up."

"I'm not sure that's such a good idea."

"Why is that, Pax?" she asked him, her voice sultry. "Have you been thinking about me? I've been thinking about you."

Paxton blew out a heavy breath. "Potter, you know I am happy with Bits, right?"

"Is that really true, Pax? Don't you ever wonder what it might have been like with us together?"

Pax's mind was racing. "You know that I do." His voice was barely more than a whisper.

"So meet me for a drink. It's just a drink."

"Fine. When?"

"Tonight?"

"Where?"

"I'll text you an address of a place in Watson Grove. I am assuming you'd prefer the busybodies of Collingswood not see us together?"

"Okay, fine. Seven o'clock?"

"See you then." After they disconnected, Pax leaned back heavily against his chair. He knew this was a bad idea. This would turn into a web of lies and he was really bad at lying. Even knowing all of that, he was excited at the prospect of seeing Potter later that night. He picked up his phone and dialed.

"Hi, babe," Bits answered in her always cheerful voice. "How's your day?"

"My day is good. Busy. How about you?"

"My day is good."

"Listen, I just got swamped with expense packages for three of my projects. I really need to work late tonight to get them entered into the system and generate the reporting to determine how far off budget we might be. Did you have anything planned for us tonight?"

"No, nothing planned. Did you want me to bring you some dinner?" Bits was always thinking of everyone else. Pax cringed, a pang of guilt making his stomach flip.

"Thank you, but I had a late lunch. I can just make a sandwich or something when I get home."

"Okay then, I'll see you later. I love you."

"I love you too, Bits." He meant it when he said it. He felt terrible about lying to her, but the pull from Potter Wendell was too strong. Pax spent the afternoon shuffling through paperwork, not accomplishing much as he wavered between feeling like a complete asshole for lying to his wife and excited by the somewhat forbidden meeting that was to occur later that evening. Around 4:30, his phone chirped. The text from Potter had an address for a bar in Watson Grove. Pax responded that he would see her there and spent the next couple of hours reminiscing about what it was like with Potter Wendell when the two were young. He had been so in love with her all those years ago. He got in the car and drove the thirty miles to Watson Grove.

Pax arrived at The Tipsy Cow, a tiny hole in-the-wall on the east side of Watson Grove at a quarter to seven. He sat in his car in the parking lot, thinking about turning around before Potter ever arrived. Before he had a chance to act, Potter pulled in and parked her Lexus next to his car. Paxton sighed, thinking how beautiful she looked as she got out of the car. She was quite the opposite of Elizabeth. Bits was a petite blonde with big brown eyes. She was casual, relaxed, friendly. Potter, on the other hand, was tall and willowy, black hair, piercing blue eyes. Her demeanor was one of class, sophistication, and all business. Paxton opened the driver's side door and stepped out to greet her.

Potter reached for Pax, embracing him tightly. He put his arms around her waist, breathing in her spicy perfume. "Hi," she said. Her voice was sultry, sexy. Potter was pleased when she came back to town to see that Pax hadn't aged at all. He was still the same handsome guy, tan from his work outdoors. His hair was still jet black and full, his eyes still sapphire blue, the only change being the crow's-feet that appeared when he smiled. That smile was still magnetic, his teeth perfectly straight and white. And he still grew a five o'clock shadow by noon.

"Hi yourself." His arms tightened around her waist, pulling her against his body. Before he knew what was happening, he felt her lips on his. Paxton knew he should pull away, but the fire in his belly wouldn't allow it. He kissed her back, softly at first and then with more hunger.

"I don't really want a drink, Pax. Come with me." She took his hand and opened the passenger door. Paxton got in and fastened his seat belt. His mind was racing, his heart pounding. Potter got in and started the car, backed out of the parking spot, and pulled onto the main road. It was only a short drive to The Amber Motel. Potter pulled in and parked. She dug in her bag, producing a key. "I already checked in."

She opened her door, sliding her long legs out of the car. Paxton sat, paralyzed by guilt. He knew if he went in the motel room with Potter that he wouldn't be able to stop himself. He would sleep with her and betray his wife. The voices, the internal argument, raged in his head. "Are you coming?"

Paxton took a deep breath as he opened the car door and stepped onto the pavement. He followed Potter up the concrete stairs, holding tightly to the iron railing. They reached room 203 and Potter unlocked the door. He followed her in as she turned on the lights, closing the door behind him.

Potter moved towards him. "Potter, this isn't a good idea." Paxton tried to resist her advances.

"I don't really feel like talking, Paxton," she said, kissing his mouth and unbuttoning his shirt. Desire overtook him. His arms went around her waist, his hands traveling to her firm rear end, stopping long enough to unbutton and unzip her skirt. It didn't take long for the clothes to come off in the frenzy of lust. There was no foreplay; the two moved right to the main event. As he entered her, Pax felt a familiarity to her touch coupled with the excitement of being with someone new. He had only been intimate with Elizabeth since the two started dating more than thirty years ago. He and Potter had slept together for years prior to their breakup. She had been Paxton's first love, the first woman he had ever been with. Things were different this time. Potter was in charge, on top, controlling the situation, and working hard at fulfilling her own needs.

Over the years Paxton had fantasized about making love to Potter, reminiscing about how great they were together. Now that he was in the moment, it wasn't anything like his fantasies. It was mechanical, cold, and selfish on her part. Potter's pleasure finally peaked. She called out his name as she crested. Paxton was just relieved it was over. There was no pleasure on his side of this equation.

"Well, that was nice, Pax." She kissed his lips and rolled onto her back. Paxton felt sick to his stomach. He got up and started to dress. "I was hoping you might stay tonight. We could have another round," she said as she ran her hands over her breasts and stomach. The thought of being with her again made Paxton shudder.

"That's not going to happen, Potter. I need you to take me back to my car."

"Oh, come on, Pax. I wanted to have some more fun."

"Get dressed, Potter, or I am calling a cab."

"Fine." She sighed and got up from the bed, starting to pull on her clothes. "I remember you being a lot more fun, Paxton."

"Yeah, I could say the same about you," he muttered as he picked up his jacket and walked out of the room, down the stairs, and to the car. Potter joined him after a minute or two, opening the driver's side door and getting into the car. Pax climbed into the passenger side and she backed out of the parking space.

"So when do you want to do this again, Pax?"

"This is never happening again, Potter. Not ever."

"Oh, we'll see about that." Her tone was one of control and manipulation. She parked next to Pax's car. He got out without a word and slammed the door to her car, unlocked the door to his car, and got into his own vehicle. She backed out and drove away, leaving Pax to wallow in his guilt and self-loathing. He sat for a moment, trying to compose himself enough to drive home. Pax started the car and noticed the time on the digital display, 8:05. In just over sixty minutes he had quite possibly destroyed his life. For what? He felt sick as he backed out and drove towards home.

It was about a quarter to nine when Paxton pulled into his garage. He dreaded going inside, feeling certain Bits would be able to see his betrayal just by looking at him. Pax went through the garage door and through the kitchen, finding Elizabeth in the living room watching TV and looking through a package of paperwork from an upcoming auction. Bits worked with Pierre Jacobs at The Age of Vintage and the two of them were preparing for an upcoming buy. "Hi, sweetie," she said.

"Hey. I am heading to the shower." He turned and walked up the stairs. Bits sighed. She picked up the phone and dialed Gavin.

"He's home. Didn't have five words to say to me and said he was going to take a shower."

"Don't read into anything, Bits. It's Paxton. He is capable of a lot of things but cheating on you just isn't one of them," Gavin tried to reassure her. He didn't know what was up with his brother, but he was confident infidelity wasn't it.

"I wouldn't be reading into things if she wasn't back in town."

"He was acting strange before she showed up, remember?" Elizabeth sighed. She really didn't know what to think. Typically they had an easy-going relationship where they were comfortable with each other and enjoyed spending time together. These last few weeks, Pax had been so distant. For the first time in her married life, Bits was worried. She really had no idea how to fix whatever was wrong and had tried several approaches to get him to open up. Nothing was working.

The Road to Regret

Elizabeth waited for Pax to come back downstairs after his shower. He never did. She finished flagging the items she wanted to go after in the auction, turned off the television and the lights, and went upstairs. Paxton was already in bed, the lights off. He was facing away from her side of the bed as close to the edge of the bed on his side as he could get without falling off. Elizabeth changed into her nightgown and crawled under the covers. She wanted to wake him, to touch him, to feel his touch. Instead, she lay still in the darkness, letting her mind spin on the awful thoughts of what could be wrong with their marriage. At some point she did sleep because when she woke the next morning, Paxton was already gone.

Paxton hardly slept that night and got up early, silently dressing and slipping out before Bits woke. He couldn't face her. When his cell phone rang early that morning, he assumed it was his wife wondering why he had left so early and without saying goodbye. It was Gavin. Bits had called him in tears; he wanted to check on Pax and see what he could find out.

"Hello?"

"Morning. How goes it?"

"Gavin, hey. What's up? It's early for you to be calling."
"I wanted to check in and say hi."

"Well, that's BS. You never call to check in and say hi."

"Okay, I wanted to talk to you about a bid I got to see what you thought, but I could have an interest in what's going on, you know."

"Send me the bid and I will look it over for you."

"Where are you? It's early."

"I am in the car on my way to the office. I'm behind on expenses on a couple of projects."

"Oh, I figured you would have caught that stuff up last night." Pax was silent. "I talked to Bits last night."

"What did she say?"

"Nothing much. Just that you were working late, and she was trying to flag the stuff she wanted to have Pierre buy in the next auction." Paxton was relieved.

"Yeah, I still have more to catch up. Look, Gavin, I need to run. If you want me to look at your bid, send me an email. I'll talk to you later." With that, Paxton hung up before Gavin even had a chance to say goodbye.

Three days later, things in Paxton's world went from bad to worse. He was exhausted, unable to sleep, and had barely spoken to Bits since his liaison with Potter. In addition, he hadn't spoken to any of his family, which was unusual, and he had not accomplished anything at work. He was relying on his foreman to put out fires on the various projects when usually he was the one who stepped in whenever there were problems. His phone rang and he answered without looking to see who it was. He instantly regretted it. "Hello?"

"Hi there." Paxton shuddered when he heard Potter's voice.

"What do you want, Potter?"

"You know what I want, Paxton. I want to know when we are getting together again."

"That's not going to happen."

"Oh really? Are you sure about that Pax? I would hate to have to have a conversation with Elizabeth about what happened the other night. I am pretty sure she would be heartbroken."

"You wouldn't do that."

"If it gets me what I want, I will do pretty much anything, Paxton. Did you not remember that about me?"

"What do you want from me, Potter?"

"Ultimately, I want you to leave your wife for me so the two of us can be together. But, for now, I could live with being the one on the side, assuming I get my fair share of your attention."

"I don't want to be with you, Potter."

"I don't believe that for an instant, Paxton. I can't imagine that you are happy with your frumpy, boring wife."

"Don't talk about her that way."

"So when can I pencil you in for another tryst?"

"Never.."

"You'll regret that, Paxton. I can make your life a living hell, and if you don't give me what I want, I will do just that." Potter hung up the phone. Paxton swallowed hard, unsure if Potter was serious in her threats to tell Elizabeth.

He went home that evening and was relieved to see that Potter had not talked to Elizabeth, at least not yet. The evening was spent as the several prior evenings had been, no communication between the two of them. Paxton was terrified that Elizabeth would find out. He decided he had to talk to someone about it and that person was his brother Drew.

After another sleepless night, Paxton again slipped out of bed, showered, dressed, and left the house before Bits awoke. He drove to Silver Sage Farm, hoping that Drew had gone to the office early. Drew was six years younger than Paxton, but like almost everyone else in the family, Drew was the person Pax could go to in a time of crisis. Now felt like the biggest crisis he had faced in a long time. As he pulled into the parking lot, he saw that Drew's parking spot was empty and his heart sank. He was finally ready to tell someone, to face what he had done, and Drew wasn't there. Pax pulled into the spot next to Drew's and sat, unsure if he should wait or go to the office. Thankfully Drew pulled into the parking lot before Paxton chose to leave.

"Hey, Pax. It's early! What are you doing here?"

"I need to talk to you about something, Drew."
"Okay, sounds serious." Drew got his bag from the trunk and pulled its strap over his shoulder.

"It is, actually." Drew looked at his brother and could see on his face that something was really wrong.

"Come inside." Drew unlocked the door to his office and held the door open for Pax. He set his bag down in the chair behind his desk and motioned for Pax to sit on the oversized sofa. "What's going on, Pax?" Paxton walked past the sofa and around the conference table to the window, looking out across the fields. The dew glinted in the early morning sun, not yet disturbed by the horses. Pax took a deep breath. He knew his brother, all of his brothers were going to be disappointed in him. "Pax, talk to me."

"I cheated on Bits."

Drew laughed.

"Nice one. Really, what's going on?" Paxton turned to face him and, at that moment, Drew knew he was serious. "Paxton . . . " Paxton sighed, pulling out one of the conference table chairs and sitting heavily.

"I cheated on Elizabeth with Potter."

"Jesus, Pax. When?"

"Four days ago. It gets worse."

"Wow, how much worse can it get, Paxton?"

"Potter is threatening to tell Elizabeth if I don't continue the affair."

"You have to tell her, Pax. It's going to be devastating enough for her. She can't hear it from someone else."

"She's going to hate me."

"Quite possibly. But she will forgive you."

"You don't know that."

"I don't; you're right. But I do know Elizabeth and have for a long time. I am betting that with some work, she will forgive you."

"Would you forgive Ange?" Drew paused, thinking about his answer.

"I would forgive Ange because I made a vow to stay with her in good times and in bad. It would take some time and we would have to work on rebuilding trust, but we would work it out."

Paxton pondered his answer. "I can't tell her. I don't know what to say."

"You need to have this come from you. I don't imagine that Potter Wendell would be very gentle in how she breaks the news."

"She's going to leave me, Drew. I fucked up my life for nothing. It was horrible. Was Potter always such a bitch?"

Drew smiled. "Um, yeah, she was. Sorry, dude."

"Look, I have a friend that is a therapist. He could recommend someone for marriage counseling if you like. It might be good to go into this with a plan you can present to Bits on how you two can fix it."

"Yeah, okay."

"When are you going to tell her?"

"I don't know. Tonight maybe?"

Drew shook his head no. "I think you should go home and do it now. You don't want to risk Potter calling her or showing up at the shop today."

Paxton sighed. He knew Drew was right. He stood to leave. "Do you hate me?"

"Come on, Pax. I could never hate you. I don't understand why this happened, but I will always be here for you and try to support you." The two shared a brotherly embrace then Paxton walked slowly to his car. He steered the car towards his house, hoping Elizabeth hadn't yet left for the shop.

Back to Reality

Paxton pulled into the garage. Elizabeth's car was still there. He turned off the ignition and sat, pondering the fact that his life was about to blow up. His phone chirped. It was a text from Drew: *Aerrick Mangum is the name of the marriage counselor. He is expecting your call for an appointment.* Aerrick and Archer Mangum were brothers, both practicing psychiatrists who decided to get out of the big city of Philadelphia and start up a practice in a more rural area. They settled in Watson Grove, starting Magnum Counseling services a few years before. Aerrick specialized in marriage counseling while Archer focused on individuals.

He took a deep breath and got out of the car then headed inside to find his wife. "Bits?" he called to her.

"Pax? What are you doing here?" she asked, coming down the stairs while putting an earring in her left ear.

"Bits, I need to talk to you about something." Elizabeth looked at her watch. She was running late, but this was the first time that he had wanted to talk about things, so she didn't care.

"Let me text Pierre and tell him I'll be late." She dug in her purse for her phone. "Okay, what's up?"

"Let's sit." He took her hand and led her to the living room. Bits sat on the sofa, her heart pounding. "Bits . . . " A thousand words ran through his head, none of them seeming right for the situation. "Bits, I've done something. Something horrible. Something I regret and something that is going to make you angry." Paxton paused, trying to maintain his composure.

"Just tell me what it is, Pax."

"I slept with someone, with Potter. Bits, I am so, so sorry." His eyes brimmed with tears.

Elizabeth stood and walked towards the picture window in their living room, trying to take in what she had heard. She wasn't totally surprised by the news, but she was taken aback at how awful the confirmation that her worst fears were true made her feel. She thought she was prepared, but now that it was happening, her heart was breaking. Paxton stood and walked towards her.

"Bits . . . "

"Please don't, Pax."

"We need to talk about this."

"We do, but I need some time. I think it would be a good idea if you went and stayed with one of your brothers for a while."

"I have a marriage counselor lined up if you are interested in that approach."

"I don't know what I want at the moment, Pax. You are going to have to give me some time to wrap my head around this. I think you should go."

"Elizabeth . . . "

"Just go." She turned and went up the stairs, closing the bedroom door behind her.

"I love you," he called after her.

Elizabeth sat on the bed, numb. She wanted to cry but couldn't. Her emotions—a jumbled mess of anger, heartbreak, grief, and jealousy—were so overwhelming that her body defaulted to feeling nothing. Once she heard the garage door close and Pax's car pull out of the drive, she walked downstairs. She picked up her bag and got in her car, heading to the shop. On her way there she called Gavin.

"Hey, Bits, good morning."

"So, I was right."

"Right about what?"

"Pax just informed me that he slept with Potter Wendell."

Gavin was stunned. "Where are you, Elizabeth?"

"I'm on my way to the shop. I have to drop off some paperwork for an auction tomorrow to Pierre. Then I am going back home, closing my door, and falling apart."

"I honestly didn't think this was possible, Bits. I am so sorry. What can I do?"

"Nothing. Come for a visit, maybe, but other than that, nothing. He suggested we go to marriage counseling."

"Is that what you want to do? Work things out with him?"

"I don't know what I want to do. I told him he had to stay somewhere else for a while. Do you think we can work things out?"

"I think that's something only you can answer, Bits. I don't know if I could forgive someone for a betrayal that big. You have to work that one out for yourself."

Meanwhile, Paxton was driving aimlessly, unsure of where to go. He called into work and let them know he would be assessing job sites for the day, but he really had no desire to visit his different project sites. He was shaken by Bits' reaction. Lack of reaction was a better description. He expected tears and yelling and fighting, not such a calm and measured response. His phone rang. It was Drew.

"Hey, checking on you."

"Well, I told her."

"And?"

"I need a place to stay awhile if that's any indication."

"You can stay with us."

"Thanks, Drew, but I think I need to be alone. I am going to stop by and see if Neal has a room I can rent for the foreseeable future."

"Did you talk to her about counseling?"

"I did, but I'm not sure she wants to go that route. She might just want to end things. I don't know. Her reaction wasn't what I expected."

"What do you mean? What were you expecting?"

"I don't know. Tears, an argument, anger, something. She was completely calm and emotionless."

"Do you want me to have Ange check on her?"

"Probably not a bad idea. My other line is ringing, I will talk to you later." Pax switched to the other line and was blasted by Gavin.

"You are a complete asshole."

"Stay out of it, Gavin."

"How could you do this to her, Pax? She has doted over you for more than thirty years and now you decide to go and fuck someone else? Potter? Really? She is such a bitch! What the fuck is wrong with you?"

"Are you done?"

"No, I'm not done. I'm just getting started."

"Well, then I am hanging up. I feel shitty enough about it without you piling on." Pax disconnected the call. Gavin tried calling him back, but it went to voicemail.

As word spread through the family, both Bits and Paxton were fielding and, in some cases, ignoring phone calls and texts. Paxton completed his rounds through the various job sites, making a halfhearted attempt to ensure all was going well. He was thankful he had a good team of foremen who could handle anything that came up while he was distracted dealing with things with Bits.

Paxton drove to The Chesterton Dulce Inn & Winery on the south side of Collingsworth. He walked into the entry of the stately limestone Victorian house that had been converted to a bed and breakfast. He rang the bell on at the front desk.

"Be right with you!" Neal called from a room upstairs. Neal Chesterton and his sister Alyson Majors ran the inn and the winery, Neal focusing on the inn and Alyson handling the winery, wine production, and events. The Chesterton house had been in their family for generations, and the brother and sister team were committed in making the house self-sustaining from a financial perspective so it could remain in the family for generations to come.

"Pax! It's great to see you, my friend. It's been too long," Neal said.

"Hey, Neal." The two men shook hands, "I was hoping you might have a room available?"

"I do. How long do you need it for?"

"I'm really not sure, Neal. Bits and I are having . . ." Neal held up his hand.

"The room is yours for as long as you need it, Pax. I'm sorry to hear about you and Bits. I could use some help with a few repairs around here. Would you be interested in trading some of your skills for room and board?"

"That would be great, Neal. Thank you!"

"Did you want to get settled now?"

"Uh, sure." Neal picked up a set of keys from behind the desk.

"Follow me." Paxton followed him through the house and out the back door.

"Neal, you don't need to put me in the cottage. Isn't that your biggest moneymaker?"

"Typically, yes, but that is where I need your help the most. There are some issues that have prevented me from being able to rent it out."

"Fair enough. I'm happy to do whatever repairs are necessary."

Neal unlocked the door to the tiny cottage and the two men entered. He showed Paxton around and pointed out some of the issues with the space.

"Here are the keys. Come and go as you please. Breakfast is served around eight in the mornings and dinner at six thirty each evening. We don't do a lunch service, but I can always rustle something up should you need it."

"Thank you, Neal. I really appreciate it."

Paxton's phone had been buzzing nonstop with texts and phone calls all morning. He didn't feel like dealing with anyone, so he had ignored them all. Sitting in the parking lot of The Golden Burger picking at his fries, he checked his messages. First, he would deal with the texts.

Jack: *I just talked to Drew. Are you okay? Do you need a place to stay? Call me.*

Angelica: *Worried about you, tried to call both of you and didn't connect with either.*

Dad: *Son, we need to talk. Please call your mother or me.*

Cindy Lewis: *Hi, Pax, could you give Gary a quick call when you get a second? He said not urgent. Thank you!*

Hank Wright: *Hey, can you take a look at the email I sent? Just want your eyes on the subcontractor bid before I approve it.*

Chance: *Tried calling. Let me know if you need to talk or if you need a place to stay.*

Jakob: *Are you okay?*

Owen: *I just heard. Call me back.*

Ryan Blankenship: *I am here if you need anything.*

Paxton sighed. He was grateful for the support of his family, but it was overwhelming at times to have that many people in your business. He responded back to Jack and let him know he was fine, had a place to stay, and would call him later that evening. Then he let Angelica know he was fine and that she should focus on supporting

Bits rather than him right now. He skipped over the text message from his father. Paxton was dreading the conversation with his parents. He also skipped over the text from Pastor Blankenship. Another conversation he wasn't looking forward to. After checking the email from Hank, he sent him a text letting him know the bid was fine and thanked him for checking before approving. He sent texts to Chance, Jakob, and Owen that were similar to what he sent to Jack. He dialed his boss, Gary Larsson.

"Paxton. How are you?"

"Good boss, good. I saw a text from Cindy that you wanted to talk to me. What can I do for you?"

"I wanted to check on you. I heard about what's happening with you and Elizabeth, and I wanted to see if you needed anything. Do you need me to cover anything for you?"

"Thank you, Gary, but no. I need the diversion of work right now to help get me through this, but I appreciate you asking."

"If you need any time or anything else, just ask, Pax."

"I will. Thank you." Paxton hung up and decided to ignore the eight voicemails. He wasn't hungry, so he gathered the garbage from his car and tossed it in the can as he left the parking lot. He wanted to reach out to Bits, to know how she was, to know his standing with her, but he was afraid of the answer. He wasn't even sure what he would say to her anyway. His apology felt so empty. He couldn't figure out a way to convey the depths of his guilt for what he had done.

Elizabeth was restless. She still hadn't had an emotional reaction to the situation with her husband. She had come home from the shop after telling Pierre she wasn't feeling well. He would find out the truth soon enough. She changed into sweatpants and a t-shirt and tidied up the house. She tried to watch TV but couldn't concentrate. She tried reading a book then a magazine but had the same problem. Her phone buzzed incessantly, but she ignored it, unable to talk about what was happening yet. Bits undressed and took a long hot shower, put on pajamas, closed the blinds and curtains in her bedroom, and crawled under the covers. Maybe she could sleep instead of having to think about things. After tossing and turning for a while, she gave up and got up to take an over-the-counter sleep aid.

Around seven that evening, Bits woke to discover Waverly sitting on the side of her bed. "Hi there."

"Hi. What are you doing here?" Bits asked her sleepily.

"Well, no one has heard from you all day. Gavin is about to charter a plane to fly down here, so I thought it would be okay to use the key and check on you. I hope that's all right?"

Bits smiled and nodded. "Of course it's okay. I'm sorry I had everyone so worried. I didn't answer my phone because it's just strange that the people I rely on in every crisis are his family."

"That's crazy, Bits. You are as much a part of this family as he is. We just want to make sure you are okay. Are you okay?"

"I honestly don't know how I am. I haven't really had any reaction. I feel like I want to cry and scream and shout, but nothing comes out."

"I'm sure it will take some time."

"He wants us to go see a marriage counselor."

"How do you feel about that?"

"I don't know. Is this fixable, Waverly?"

"I can't answer that for you, Bits. You have to decide if you want to work it out or end things. Counseling might be a good way to find out."

"Yeah, maybe."

"Are you hungry? I brought some food and popped it in the fridge."

"Thank you, but no, not very hungry. You should go home and take care of Chance and the girls. I'm fine."

"You're sure? You could come and stay with us for as long as you like."

"You are very sweet, but I promise I am fine. I will reach out to everyone over the next couple of days. I just need some time before I talk about it, you know?"

"You take all the time you need. And I am just a phone call away." Waverly stood to leave and Bits got up to walk her out. They shared a quick embrace before Waverly headed out the door and to her car. Before backing out of the driveway, she sent a group text letting everyone know that Bits was fine.

Paxton tossed and turned for the majority of the night. He finally gave up, getting up well before sunrise. After showering and dressing, he sat down to make a list of projects and supplies he would need to fix up the little cottage he was calling home. The cottage was actually the old carriage house. The outside was painted a pale sea-foam green with white trim. Paxton noted that it could use a fresh coat of paint outside as well as the replacement of a few trim boards. There were two suites, the Daffodil Room, which was downstairs, and the Wisteria Suite, which had its own entrance upstairs. Both rooms were bright and sunny with large French doors.

Pax was staying downstairs in the room done with shades of yellows and pale greens. It had a stone fireplace with a gas insert, a king-sized four-poster bed, nice amenities like a small refrigerator, microwave, coffee maker, and flat-screen TV. The antique furniture was beautiful, provided by Pierre. There was also an oversized bathroom with a huge tub and separate shower. Pax made his punch list for the lower level room.

Upstairs in the Wisteria Suite, the amenities were much the same. The room was done in pale purples and grays; it had a very romantic and cozy feel. Paxton noted some water damage to the ceiling. He would have to climb onto the roof and do an assessment at some point soon. He continued making his notes and then went back downstairs to estimate the materials for each repair. His phone rang. "Hello?"

"When can we get together, Paxton?"

"Go to hell, Potter. Stop calling me. We won't ever be getting together again."

"Oh? Do I need to be making a phone call to Elizabeth?" Potter's voice was sickeningly sweet.

"Feel free, she already knows everything."

Potter was silent, annoyed at not having leverage over him any longer. "And did you tell her you are leaving her for me?"

Paxton laughed. "That wouldn't happen in a million years, Potter. Elizabeth and I are going to be fine." Paxton wished he felt as confident as he sounded.

"We'll see about that." She disconnected the call. Paxton sighed, dreading whatever awful thing that Potter was going to think up next.

Pax walked the short distance to the house to have breakfast. "Morning, Neal," he said as he picked up a plate and helped himself to some eggs and sausage.

"How did you sleep?"

"I didn't, but not because of the accommodations."

"I understand. I'm sorry you are having troubles."

"Thanks. I made a punch list of items I want to tackle in the cottage. I will head to Barber later today and pick up some supplies so I can get started this weekend."

"There's no rush, Pax."

"I am happy to have something to keep me busy." Pax sat at one of the small tables in the corner of the dining room and stared at his breakfast. His cell phone chirped, indicating a new text message.

Bits: *Make an appointment with the counselor for early next week. I'm not saying it will fix anything, but it can't hurt to see what he has to say. Let me know what time and where.*

Paxton smiled. It was the most hopeful he had felt in days. He scrolled through his texts from Drew to find the number for the marriage counselor and dialed.

"Aerrick Mangum."

"Um, hi, Dr. Mangum. My name is Paxton Cooke. I got your name from my brother, Drew. I would like to make an appointment for my wife and myself to come in next week if possible?" Pax couldn't believe how nervous he was.

"It's Aerrick, please. Dr. Mangum is so formal. Let me look at my book." There was a pause while he checked his schedule. "Does Tuesday at ten o'clock work for you?"

"Yes, we can make that work. Where is your office?"

"I am at 10 Lavender Lane in Watson Grove. What is your wife's name?"

"Elizabeth."

"All right then, Paxton. I will see the two of you on Tuesday."

"Thank you." And just like that the appointment was made. Pax was surprised and relieved that he didn't have to answer a hundred questions over the phone, that he didn't have to say out loud that he was an adulterer and that was the reason they needed counseling. He knew it was coming though. On Tuesday, he would likely have to speak his sins out loud. Paxton texted the information to Bits and then went to his first job site to check on the progress there. He pushed away from the table, leaving an almost full plate of food. He really didn't have much of an appetite.

Elizabeth was up and out early as well, unlocking the shop then going through the mail and packages. While she waited for Pierre, she decided to do a dusting of the store. She wiped down the back first, removing the treasures from each shelf, wiping down the shelves, and then gently and carefully returning them to their spots. She had just about made it to the midpoint of the store when Pierre came in through the back. He had a trailer full of new items they had purchased at the auction the day before.

"Elizabeth! I didn't expect to see you today. How are you doing, my dear?" It was evident from his expression that he had heard the rumors.

"I'm fine, Pierre. Thanks for asking. Let's get that trailer unloaded! I can't wait to see what we purchased so I can decide what to dress the windows with. I thought I would change both displays today."

"All right, then. To the alley." Elizabeth was thankful that Pierre didn't push her to talk about things. She wasn't sure she could keep herself together if she had to talk about what Paxton had done. Anger about the situation was now brewing deep in her gut. Elizabeth wondered what Tuesday would be like. She had never envisioned her and Pax needing counseling.

The weekend was spent with both Pax and Bits trying to keep busy. Paxton was making good progress on repairs to the cottage and Neal was thrilled to have the help.

Bits had put together two stunning window displays using a combination of items from the auction and some things they had on hand. She spent the weekend reorganizing the shop to accommodate the additional inventory.

They both spent the weekend fielding messages and calls from family and friends. Monday dragged on for both of them as they anticipated what the next day had to offer.

Paxton was the first to arrive on Tuesday. The receptionist, LeTrecia Anderson, greeted him. "Welcome! Aerrick is just finishing up with another couple. Have a seat and he will be right with you."

Paxton sat in one of the overstuffed leather chairs in the lobby. Bits arrived shortly after and sat on the sofa with little more than a hello to Pax. He studied her as she thumbed through a magazine. She looked tired and a bit frightened or maybe nervous. The door to Dr. Aerrick Mangum's office opened and a couple filed out into the lobby. The woman was dabbing her eyes with a tissue; the man was expressionless. Both Bits and Paxton squirmed in their seats.

"Mr. & Mrs. Cooke, I'm Aerrick. It's a pleasure to meet you both," he said as he shook hands with each of them. "Please, come in. Make yourselves comfortable."

Aerrick was a bit of a contradiction in terms. He was a tall stocky black man with an ominous physical presence, yet when he spoke, his voice was deep and warm and inviting, putting most people at ease. "So, what brings the two of you in today?" Both Paxton and Elizabeth were silent, neither wanting to say the words. Aerrick let the silence continue for a few minutes. "We're going to have some challenges making progress if neither of you is willing to talk about the problem." Again, silence.

"I cheated on my wife." Paxton's voice was barely audible.

"I see. And when did this take place?"

"Two weeks ago." Aerrick was making notes on a yellow legal pad.

"And is the affair continuing?"

"What? No! And it wasn't an affair. It was a one-time thing. A stupid mistake."

"Was it with someone you knew or a stranger?"
"Someone I knew." Paxton mumbled the words.

"Someone you were previously involved with or someone you had never been intimate with?"

Paxton paused.

"Previously involved," Bits blurted out, the anger in her voice palpable.

"Is this the first time the marriage has dealt with infidelity?"

"Yes," Paxton said.

"Elizabeth?"

"Oh, sorry, yes."

"How long have the two of you been married?"

"Thirty-three years," Elizabeth answered.

"And how long did you two date before you got married?"

"A little over a year."

"Okay then, that is all the questions I have at the moment. Let's talk about how you both are feeling." Again, the doctor was met with stoic expressions and no words. "Elizabeth?"

Bits sighed as she thought about what she wanted to say. "How am I feeling? I am not even sure how to put it in words. Angry, betrayed, heartbroken, ashamed." Her voice caught on that last one.

"Ashamed? Why are you feeling ashamed?" Aerrick probed with a warm, gentle voice.

"I know I shouldn't care about what other people think, but do you have any idea how embarrassing it is to be the woman who couldn't keep her man? What is wrong with me that he had to do this? Am I a bad wife or just bad in bed? It feels like that is what everyone is thinking."

Paxton cringed. He knew she was angry and betrayed and that he had broken her heart, but he had no idea that she felt shame.

"Paxton, how are you feeling?" Aerrick asked.

"Worse than I was a minute ago. You have nothing to be ashamed about, Bits. This is all on me. Why I did what I did was not in any way because of you." Tears brimmed in Paxton's eyes. "Please, Bits, I need you to understand that."

"You don't get to need me to feel a certain way, Paxton. I feel like I feel." Her words were harsh. Paxton looked at his hands in his lap, at a loss for words.

"Paxton, would you like to continue to share how you feel?"

"Not particularly."

"I hate this," Bits said, "I hate that you did this to us and that we have to sit here in front of a perfect stranger and air our dirty laundry. No offense, Dr. Mangum."

"None taken, and it's Aerrick, please."

"I hate that you threw away almost forty years. I have been with you for longer than I have been without you, and you just threw it away. And for what? A good fuck?" Bits was feeling the fury, the emotions that had eluded her since all of this happened. Paxton sat stoic in the chair, not making eye contact with either his wife or the doctor. Aerrick let the silence linger in the hopes that Paxton would speak. He did not.

"We are getting close to our time being up for today. Let's chat about whether the two of you would like to come back. If so, how often?"

"I would come back," Elizabeth said softly.

"Me too," Pax said, his voice a whisper.

"Okay. I suggest once a week until we get some things worked out. Will that work for both of you?" Both nodded yes. "This same time each week?" Again, both nodded.

"I have one more question for you. Are the two of you staying at the same place at the moment?"

"No, I have a room at The Chesterton."

"Okay, that's good, at least for the time being. Let's see how things go." Aerrick stood, Bits and Pax following suit. "Thank you both for coming in. I will see you next week." Aerrick opened the door leading to the lobby and welcomed his next patients. Elizabeth walked quickly to her car, not wanting to give Paxton a chance to say a thing. She didn't need to worry because he didn't know what to say to her anyway. He watched as she drove away, wondering if they would ever find their way back to the way things used to be.

As Elizabeth drove home, the elusive tears finally came. Once home she showered, put on pajamas, and crawled into bed. She texted Pierre letting him know she wouldn't be in and texted Waverly to let her know the appointment was fine and that she was going to turn off her phone and take a nap.

Paxton's phone rang on his way home as well. He sighed when he saw the number but still answered. "Hi, Dad."

"Paxton, we have been trying to reach you for days now."

"I know. As you can imagine, things here have been pretty crazy." There was a long pause from Cord Cooke's end of the phone. "Look, Dad, I know what you are going to say and you don't need to. I am already disappointed in myself enough without you piling on." Again a long pause from his father.

"Are you trying to fix this?"

"I am. I just left the marriage counselor's office, in fact."

"Where are you staying? With Jack? Jakob?"

"No, Dad. I took a room at The Chesterton Dulce Inn. I am trading some work on the cottage over there for room and board for now."

"Why did you do this, son? Cookes aren't cheaters. We raised you better than this." Paxton felt the sting of his father's words as if he were eight years old again.

No matter how old you are, you hate to disappoint your parents.

"I don't have an answer for that, Dad. I wish I did. Maybe the counseling will help me figure out why."

"Do you want us to come down there?"

"It's always great to see you, Dad. But you don't need to make a special trip because of this. Both Elizabeth and I are fine. We have lots of support. But thank you for offering." The two men finished their call. The conversation wasn't as bad as Paxton had envisioned, but he was glad it was over.

The next two weeks were more of the same for Pax and Bits. Both were going through the motions at work and wading through the texts, emails, and phone calls from those who were concerned about them. Both were emotionally exhausted by the soul-baring and somewhat brutal counseling sessions with Dr. Mangum.

As they left their third session, they walked to the parking lot together. While emotions were still running high between them, they were at least able to make small talk without it feeling quite so uncomfortable. "Why don't you have dinner with me at the inn on Friday night?" Paxton suggested.

Elizabeth's first reaction was to say no, but she decided that if they were really going to try to get back to where they were before Potter Wendell, she had to do some things that might be uncomfortable. "Okay, sure. What time?"

Paxton was pleasantly surprised. "Seven? Does that work?"

"Sure, see you then." She got in the car and closed the door behind her. For some reason, her heart was pounding. Elizabeth was both dreading and looking forward to Friday night.

Elizabeth sighed as she changed into her third outfit. Nothing she had tried on looked right. The black and blue dress was a favorite of Paxton's, and since she was just about out of time, she was going with it. She found shoes and jewelry, sprayed on some perfume, and checked her hair and makeup before heading out the door.

Paxton was nervous as well. Neal had set them a lovely table for two in the dining room. He had offered to do a special table in the Daffodil Room where Pax was staying, but Paxton felt like that might send the wrong message to Bits. He knew they needed to start slow, to go slow.

Paxton waited in the lobby for Bits to arrive. He was nervous, anxious they wouldn't have anything to talk about over dinner. He took in a sharp breath as she came through the front door. "You look amazing!" he said as he kissed her cheek.

"Thank you."

Paxton took her hand and led her to their table. There was only one other couple in the dining room, so it was quiet with soft piano music playing over the speakers in the ceiling.

"This is nice. I haven't been in here in years!"

"I know. I hadn't either. They have quite an operation over here with Neal running the inn, and Alyson running the winery and doing all the events. It's a busy little place." Their bit of nervous awkwardness was broken by Neal bringing them menus and water.

"Elizabeth! So nice to see you! You look lovely."

"Thank you, Neal. It's nice to see you too."

"Can I get either of you something besides water to drink?"

"I would love a glass of merlot," Bits answered.

"A beer for me, Neal." Neal went off to the kitchen to get the drinks.

"How was the rest of your week? Things busy at the store?"

"My week was fine. The store is good. We are preparing for another auction, one that is quite large, so I have been buried in catalogs. We are also helping a new funeral home in Watson Grove with their furnishing needs, so yes, it's busy. How about you? Projects moving along okay?"

"Yeah. We have three underway and another starting up next week. Things are going pretty smoothly I guess. No complaints." Neal returned with their drinks and took their orders, beef tips for Pax and a Cornish game hen for Bits.

"I miss you. I miss this, talking about our day." Paxton had gained a much greater appreciation for what the two of them had together over the last few weeks. Elizabeth smiled but said nothing. She missed him too, but she was still so angry and hurt she couldn't say the words.

Neal brought their meals. Their small talk over dinner felt comfortable and familiar. They shared food from each other's plates. In many ways, it was as if nothing had happened. After the dinner dishes were cleared, Neal brought them after-dinner coffees and a chocolate souffle with two spoons. "I know you didn't order this, but you need it. Trust me," he said with a grin. Both of them dug into the warm, soft, gooey chocolate.

"Oh, good lord," Elizabeth said, "this is heavenly." Paxton smiled. For the first time in a while, she actually looked happy. Paxton's phone rang; it was Jack.

"Hey, Jack, what's up?"

"Where are you?"

"I'm at the inn just finishing dinner with Bits. Why?"

"Have you looked outside lately?"

"No, what's going on?"

"It's an icy mess out here. Penni and I are on our way home from the fall festival. Jakob and Shiloh took a different route. Brax, Kylie, and Rowan are somewhere on their way home too. You shouldn't go anywhere and don't let Elizabeth drive home."

"Okay. Thanks for the call. Be careful and text me when you guys get home."

"What's going on?" Elizabeth asked, concerned.

"Evidently, we are in the midst of an ice storm. Jack says the roads are a mess and I shouldn't let you drive." Neal stopped at the table to refill coffee and waters. "Neal, Bits might need a room for the night. Apparently, the weather is atrocious out there."

"Of course! Let me get you a key. Make yourself at home, Elizabeth."
"Thank you, Neal." He refilled the cups and went back to the kitchen.

"It can't be that bad, Pax. I'm sure I can make it home."

"It's pretty bad if Jack called. Let's go outside and take a look." They went through the lobby door to find the sidewalks, trees, cars, and pavement coated in ice. "You're not driving home, Bits." She nodded. Neal brought her the key and Paxton walked her to the staircase.

"I don't remember an ice storm this bad ever!" Bits exclaimed.

"It's bad and there was nothing in the forecast." Once at the staircase, there was a bit of awkwardness as the two tried to figure out a way to gracefully end the evening.

"Thanks, Pax. It was a lovely dinner. I will see you in the morning."

"Sleep well."

Back in his room, Paxton was feeling more upbeat about things between them. The evening had gone well. He changed his clothes and flipped on the television to a late night talk show.

There was a knock at the door. It was Jakob . . .

CHANCE

Empty Nests

Chance looked around Jack's back yard taking inventory. He was always taking inventory, comparing himself to his brothers. Chance had always had deep-seated insecurities. Part of that was just an aspect of his personality, and part of it was the result of his stoic, unemotional, demanding father who had high expectations that Chance felt he could never live up to.

His brothers were all more successful than he was. Paxton managed several construction crews and was an integral part of the success of Timberline Construction. Gavin was an architect, heading for partner in the prominent Chicago firm where he worked. Drew was the manager of a thriving thoroughbred horse farm, running all the operations with dozens of people reporting to him. Jakob had built his landscaping business from four or five yards to customers in three towns, a fleet of equipment, and teams of workers. Owen, the youngest Cooke, was the handsome, charming professor of fine arts at the University of Illinois in Chicago. And then there was Jack. Perfect Jack. Jack was two years younger than Chance. He was a doctor, the career military officer, and the perfect son in his father's eyes. Jack, the brother with whom he had the ongoing rift. An almost fifteen-year stalemate.

What Chance failed to see were all the challenges his brothers were facing. He didn't have the kind of relationships with them that allowed them to share with him.

Chance had been married to Waverly for thirty-four years. High-school sweethearts, they had married when Chance was eighteen and she was nineteen. They tried for many years to have children, finally conceiving via fertility treatments. Their twin daughters, Kylie and Cassie, were seventeen and preparing to graduate from high school. Kylie was the extrovert with a huge circle of friends. She was going to Georgia to study art and had been accepted at the Atlanta Institute of Art on a full scholarship. Her artistic talents outweighed her mediocre grades. Cassie, on the other hand, was a bit more introverted. She was much more content to study and read rather than socialize, and her grades reflected that. She had been accepted at several Ivy League schools, settling on Harvard, where she would start her pre-med studies in the fall.

The sisters were lovely. Both had long dark blonde hair and their father's blue eyes. Both took after their mother with their peaches and cream complexions. Both girls had boyfriends. Cassie was dating the bookish class president and valedictorian Rafe Roberts, and Kylie was seeing Rowan Cresswell, the tall and lanky basketball star.

Chance and Waverly owned three thousand acres of farmland which Chance used for corn. He was the main supplier of corn to Aegis Distillery, a small bourbon producer with its facilities in Watson Grove, located thirty-one miles from Collingswood. In his eyes, being a farmer never stacked up to the successes of his brothers.

It was uncomfortable for him to be at Jack's retirement party. The two of them had been angry with each other for so long now that the reason had almost become unimportant. Now that Jack was back in the same town, the issues would have to be dealt with, something that Chance was dreading. He was incredibly envious of Jack. The doctor, the career military man, the one with a back yard full of friends. Chance took a swig of his water, wishing it was a beer. He didn't have the yearning very often. He knew he needed to go to a meeting and get his head on straight where drinking was concerned. He did not want to fall off the wagon.

Let Bygones Be

Chance was not looking forward to the reunion with Jack and Razor Drake. He had a sinking feeling that some crazy revelation was going to occur when the three of them got together the following day. He struggled to concentrate at work, finally giving up and heading home. Waverly had made a nice dinner for him and the girls, but he wasn't hungry. Chance excused himself and went upstairs to shower. Waverly came up to check on him. "Sweetheart? Are you okay? Are you coming down with something?"

"No, I'm fine. I'm just tired. I didn't sleep well last night."

"Okay, if you are sure."

"I'm going to turn in early. I'm fine, Waverly." He gave her shoulders a gentle squeeze as he kissed her on the forehead. She went back downstairs to clean up the dinner dishes. Chance showered, changed into lounge pants and a t-shirt, and climbed into bed. He tossed and turned, desperate to sleep yet not able to turn off his mind. He couldn't come up with any reason why Razor Drake would show up out of the blue and want to meet with both him and Jack.

As Chance heard the words come out of Razor's mouth, the words that if spoken years ago would have changed the course of his life, numbness overtook him. An overwhelming jumble of emotions all culminated into a breathless void. The first thought that went through his mind was that he needed a drink. His hand stroked his stubbly beard, a gesture he made when he was deep in thought or angry. His blue-green eyes stared with fury at Razor Drake. "Do you realize what you've done? What you did to me? You ruined my military career, destroyed my life, Razor. My wife, my kids, my family, they all had to deal with this. I have spent the last fifteen years thinking I killed one of my best friends. My brother has hated my guts for the last fifteen years based on a lie." He spat the words, anger evident in his voice. "How could you do this?" Chance stormed out of the diner, momentarily disoriented, not remembering where he parked the car. He found his vehicle, got in, and slammed the door. Without a destination in mind, he drove.

He drove out of town, his head spinning. How could this be happening? He felt relief which, in turn, made him feel guilt. Chance turned on the radio hoping that the music would distract him. He listened for a few miles and then switched it off, finding it more of an annoyance than a distraction. His mind was flooded, jumbled as he continued his drive. Without realizing it, he had driven the path of his past, finding himself pulling into the parking lot of The Tipsy Cow in Watson Grove. It was his old stomping ground before he went to rehab. Chance was afraid. This was the first time his sobriety felt tenuous. Sure, there had been struggles. There were the daily battles of wanting a drink, but this felt different. This was a need, a deep desire to drink until he could no longer feel. Shaken, he backed out of the parking lot and drove back towards Collingswood. He picked up his cell phone and dialed his brother.

"Hey, Chance, what's up?" Drew's voice was cheerful in his ear.

"Can I stop by? I need to talk to you about something."

"Chance, are you okay?"

"I am just leaving Watson Grove. I could stop by your office in about fifteen minutes. Will you be free?" Drew knew it was serious by the tone of his voice.

"I'll be here. Drive safely, Chance." Chance disconnected and drove the back roads to Silver Sage Farms.

"What's going on?" Drew asked as Chance came in the door of his office. Chance brought his brother up to speed, filling him in on the details of the conversation with Razor Drake and his road trip to the bar.

"I'm scared, Drew. I haven't wanted a drink this bad in years. I don't know what to do. Should I check myself in somewhere?" Drew pondered the question. He was unsure how to answer.

"If you think you are going to slip, then yes. But, the fact that you drove away from the bar instead of parking and going in makes me think you are more in control than you're giving yourself credit for."

Chance nodded. "Okay. I will give it a couple of days and see if this craving goes away. I don't know how to feel. Guilty that I'm happy it was someone else? How fucked up is that? Happy I didn't kill him? One of my best friends is still dead. This won't bring him back."

"I think it's completely normal to feel like that. I would be relieved, not guilty, to know it wasn't me. What did Jack have to say about the whole thing?"

"I didn't give him a chance to say anything. Once Razor said what he came to say, I left. I have no idea what Jack is thinking. Maybe now this stupid rift can be over. Do you think?"

"Is that what you want?"

"That's what I have always wanted. I just didn't know how to get there. He was so angry about Doug. We've missed out on a lot in each other's lives."

"I think you need to tell him, Chance. You two can start fresh."

Drew's phone rang. "Hey, Jack."

"Have you heard from Chance?"

"I have. He's here with me."

"Thank God. How is he?"

"Pissed, relieved, rattled. About how you would expect him to be. How are you?"

"Not great, but I'll get through it. Can you stop by my place for a beer tomorrow afternoon? Linc and Clio will be here. I'd like to talk to you about what's happening, but I only have the energy to go through it once for both you and Linc."

"Sure. I will wrap up early and head your way."

Chance was doing all the right things: attending meetings regularly, staying in constant contact with his sponsor, leaning on Waverly and Drew for encouragement and support. There might be an end to this dark tunnel he was in, and he might make it out the other end without falling off the wagon and having a drink.

Work was going well. There was some discussion happening between Aegis Distillery and Chesterton Winery about a merger of sorts. Aegis would take over and expand the grape crop while Alyson Majors would take over running marketing and events for both the distillery and the wine brand. Rex Aegis, the distillery owner had spoken to Chance the week before about managing the grape crop for him in addition to the corn.

Chance dove into the research, trying to get himself prepared in case that became a reality. He met with Alyson to discuss the personnel she already had on staff and made a list of how they might need to augment that team should they significantly expand the acreage of grapes. Thankfully she already employed someone with extensive viticulture experience. Chance's role wouldn't be focused on the vines themselves but more on the logistical efficiencies of getting such a large volume of grapes from vine to bottle. He was excited at the prospect of the new challenge and hoped that Rex and Alyson were able to work out a deal that was good for both of them.

The Road to Tragedy

The next few weeks were some of the happiest that Chance had known. He had navigated through the challenges of staying sober. He felt lighter; his burden had been lifted. Things with Jack were going well. The two were talking often, having lunch together. He was happy to be reconnecting with his brother. Chance had done some reexamining of his life, realizing that he wasn't the failed man that he had spent years creating in his mind. He had a good life, a wife he loved, two amazing daughters, and a supportive extended family. He had missed realizing how blessed he was for all of those years.

He pulled in the driveway after a full day of work, anxious to be home with his wife and daughters. Chance walked through the front door, breathing in the scent of beef stew and homemade bread as he entered. He went to the kitchen and found his wife tidying up after cooking. "Hi, sweetheart," he said as he nuzzled her neck from behind. Waverly turned off the water and spun around to face her husband, kissing him.

"Hi, yourself," she said, "Hungry?"

"I am, but maybe it can wait?" Chance had a sly grin on his face as his hands softly caressed her hips and bottom. Waverly smiled. The two of them had reconnected in the last few weeks and they were spending a lot of time in the bedroom. She adjusted the burner on the stove to leave the stew on simmer and took Chance's hand. He followed her into their room, closing and locking the door. They had already had a close call of being caught by one of their daughters, which would have been embarrassing for everyone concerned. As he made love to his wife, he felt a closeness that had been missing between them for a very long time. Part of the challenge of a reawakening is that it's difficult not to have regrets. Chance tried to stay focused on the present and enjoy the feelings and connections, but in the back of his mind, the constant weight of remorse for the time lost and the pain caused to his family and friends lingered.

That Friday felt like any other day. Chance had no idea that this day would change the course of his life significantly. Waverly was working late, trying to finish a grant proposal for funding for parks and recreation. Since she was going to be late, Chance called Rex and offered to work the Aegis booth at the fall festival.

"Are you sure, Chance?" Rex asked, surprised by the call. "That doesn't really seem like it would be your thing."

"I'm sure."

"Well, okay then, we would love to have you there." Chance showered, changed, and headed for Barber. On the way, he found himself singing along with the radio, something he hadn't done in years. He was happier than he had been in a long time.

Chance spent the afternoon chatting with booth visitors and teasing his coworkers. He chatted with Jakob, Jack, and Shiloh, and met Penni for the first time. He visited Kylie at the Discovery Gallery Arts Center booth, reminding her of her 11:00 p.m. curfew.

"Yes, Dad, I know, I know." Kylie gave her father a quick squeeze before he walked through the crowd back to the Aegis booth. The team there hung out for the next hour or two then the weather conditions deteriorated. The decision was made to close up shop. Chance called Kylie who told him that she, Rowan, and Brax were leaving as well, and she would see him at home shortly. Chance thought nothing of it as the two shared their father and daughter "I love you's" and disconnected.

Chance got in the truck and headed towards Collingswood. His cell rang. He answered, hoping it was Kylie. "Hey, have you left yet?" Jack asked.

"Yeah, I am on 441. Where are you?" said Chance.

"We are on 74. It's awful."
"Pretty awful this way as well."

"Jakob and Shiloh went that way too. What about Kylie? Is she with you?"

"No, she was riding home with Rowan and Brax. If I would have known it was going to get this bad, I would have made them ride with me."

"I'm sure they will be fine. I am going to drop Penni off at her place and head home. I will check in later. Drive safe."

Chance focused on the road. His old rear-wheel-drive farm truck wasn't cut out for these conditions. He made the tense drive home and was relieved when he pulled in to find both Waverly's and Cassie's vehicles in the garage. "Waverly?" he called as he opened the door.

"It's crazy out there. I am so glad you're home."

"Where's Cassie?"

"She's upstairs sleeping, fighting off a headache." Chance put his arms around Waverly, holding her tight.

"Kylie is with Rowan and Brax. They should be right behind me." Chance was worried. As time went by without the arrival of their daughter, they went from worried to panicked to frantic. Kylie wasn't answering her cell phone. Neither was Rowan nor Brax. No one had heard from or seen them. They weren't at any of their friends' homes. Cassie was frantically checking with friends and family to see if anyone had heard from her sister or her cousin. Nothing.

There was a moment of relief as headlights came down the driveway. Chance let out a long sigh, thinking his daughter had arrived home safely. It was then he realized the car belonged to the sheriff's department and his stomach dropped.

DREW

Still a Romance

Drew smiled as he watched his wife from across the back yard of his brother's house. Angelica was laughing at something Jack had said. After all the years they had been together, Drew still thought she was the most beautiful woman around. The two had met when Drew was in the third grade and Ange was in the second. They had been best friends throughout grade school and junior high. They started dating in high school, married when Drew was twenty and Ange nineteen. Braxton had come along six years later.

Brax had his father's good looks and his ability to talk to people. He was somewhat unsure what career choice he wanted to make, resulting in Braxton wandering a bit after graduating high school. He had tried several jobs, none of them lasting very long. He surprised everyone by enrolling in the veterinary technician program at the community college in Barber. Shortly after starting to work for Shiloh his life started taking some direction. Braxton was newly single after deciding to break up with Karina Scott when she left for college. He was not the type to do long-distance dating.

Like all the Cooke brothers, Drew had dark hair, blue eyes, and handsome features. It was evident that he and his brothers were related. They all looked quite similar to the patriarch of the family, Cordero Cooke, who was tall and broad, a foreboding figure with a commanding presence. His dark hair had some grey but not much, his eyes an icy blue. A full and heavy mustache covered a kind, rarely seen smile.

Drew had worked at the Silver Sage Farm when he was in high school, mucking out stalls and doing whatever chores needed to be done. Gerald Larsson, the owner of the farm, took Drew under his wing, grooming him to run the operation.

Angelica had always loved to cook and bake. She worked part-time for the local bakery and helped out with larger catering jobs when needed. The two of them had the marriage that most envied, an easy friendship and a passionate romance steeped in the history of a lifetime together.

Drew was the keeper of secrets. He was the one that his brothers, his friends, his coworkers came to for advice because he was the listener, the voice of reason. He was considered the nicest Cooke. It was a title he both hated and loved. Drew was very much entangled in the lives of his family and his friends. As they came to him for advice, he couldn't help but take on their burdens. He worried about them when they were going through hard times. He was irritated with them when they didn't listen. He celebrated in their triumphs. The consequence of that entanglement resulted in a heavy load for one man to carry.

Drew knew how lucky he was to have a happy marriage where there were hardly ever arguments or harsh words exchanged, a well-adjusted kid, and a pretty easy life overall. He was thankful for that. He was happy his brother was back in town. If Drew had it his way, his parents, Owen, and Gavin would be much closer as well.

Having them closer meant being more involved and feeling more in control.

"You still love her as much as the day you married her, don't you?" Father Casey asked with a smile.

"More maybe," Drew said, still watching his wife interact with her sisters-in-law. Ange, Bits, and Waverly were a bit of a tribe. They were close friends. The friendships were hatched before they married into the Cooke family but were further strengthened by necessity. They were each other's salvation because marrying into a family with seven brothers and a rigid patriarch was no easy task. They stuck together and all were relieved not to have to deal with Jakob's ex, Delilah, now that the two of them had split. She was forever trying to cause problems within the family.

It wasn't until several days after the retirement party that things began to spiral downward for Drew. For no reason in particular, Drew was angry. He was annoyed and short with his coworkers and with Angelica, which was very unusual. She tried to talk to him, to find out what it was that had him so worked up, but he just became angrier, and the two left the conversation upset.

"I have no idea what's going on with him," Angelica lamented over lunch with Bits. "He never acts this way. I'm worried."

"I'm sure it's just a bad mood or maybe something at work. Try not to take it personally, Ange. He will be calling with an apology any minute." But he didn't call to apologize. In fact, Angelica didn't hear from him until he walked through the door that evening. His mood hadn't changed; he skipped dinner and went to bed.

The next morning, Drew was still in a foul temper. He picked at his breakfast and hardly spoke to Angelica. He showered and dressed and left with a short and distant goodbye. After he left, Ange dressed and drove to Jack's office. This behavior was so unusual for Drew, she thought he might be ill.

"Hey Ange! What brings you by this early?" Jack asked as she came into the lobby of his clinic.

"I think something is wrong with Drew, Jack. He is acting really strange."

"Strange in what way?" Jack motioned to the black leather love seat as he sat on the matching sofa. Ange sat heavily, feeling like she was carrying the weight of the world.

"He is angry about something. He has been short with me, really short with me. He skipped dinner last night. I talked to one of the girls at the farm when she came into the bakery, and he has been rather short with people at work too. Something's not right, Jack. I am really worried."

"Try not to get too worked up, Ange. I will check in on him later this afternoon, okay? I am sure there is a simple explanation for what's going on." Ange knew Jack was trying to make her feel better. It wasn't working. "I will call you after he and I have had a chance to chat."

Ange stood to leave. "Thanks, Jack." He stood and gave her a quick hug. It was unusual for the two of them to be arguing. Jack hoped it was nothing serious happening with his brother. He would drive over to the horse farm after his last patient at three o'clock.

Jack never had the chance to drive to Silver Sage Farm. It was just after two o'clock when Drew came bursting through the door of his clinic. "Jack," he was breathing heavily, sweating, and clutching at his chest, "I think I am having a heart attack." Jack had just finished with his one-thirty patient and didn't have anyone scheduled until two thirty. He helped Drew into the exam room.

"Try to stay calm," Jack said as he listened to Drew's chest and took his blood pressure. "Try to slow down your breathing." He hooked Drew up to cardiac monitoring equipment, surveying the information the machine was producing. Jack reached into a drawer and pulled out a paper bag. "Breathe into the bag, Drew. Slow, deep breaths. You're okay." Jack helped Drew hold the bag as he followed his brother's instructions. The pain in his chest subsided and Drew's breathing returned to normal. "You're okay, Drew. It wasn't a heart attack."

"Then what the hell was it?" Drew asked between breaths.

"It was a panic attack, Drew. Your stress levels got so high that it triggered an autonomic reaction in your body. Everything is okay." Jack was still trying to soothe Drew, to calm him and get his blood pressure and heart rate back to normal levels.

"Will it happen again?"

"It could. If you don't deal with the source of the stress you are feeling, it could happen again."

"I'm not stressed out, Jack."

"Your body says otherwise. I am going to refer you to a great therapist I know."

"You think I need therapy? What do I have to be stressed out about, Jack? I have a great wife, a great marriage, a great kid, a great job. There is nothing stressful there."

"Yes, but you are the one all of us go to for advice. You worry about everyone and take on everyone's problems like they are your own. There are a lot of us, Drew. It's a heavy burden. Give Archer a call. I think you will like him. Now, do you want me to call Ange and have her come pick you up?"

"No, I'm fine. I am going to head home and go to bed. I am exhausted."

"It's a common aftereffect from an attack like that. Get some rest and I will check on you later this evening."

The Bumpy Road to Fewer Burdens

Archer Mangum watched as his new patient Drew Cooke squirmed uncomfortably in the large overstuffed chair in his office. "Why did you come to see me today, Drew?"

"I feel overwhelmed. My brother, the doctor, recommended you."

"Overwhelmed by what?"

"By what's happening in the lives of my family. I don't know how to help them."

"Help them with what?"

"Help them fix their problems."

"Why do you need to help them?"

"Because they all came to me for help."

"And why do you think that is?"

"I don't know. Because I am the nice one. The one who everyone tells their troubles and their secrets. It's been that way since I was a child."

"I see. Who do you tell your troubles to?"

"I don't really have any troubles, I guess."

"Everyone has troubles, Drew."

"What about your wife? Do you share your troubles with her?"

"I don't really, but I could. I could share anything with her, but I don't like to burden her."

"What about your brother? The doctor."

"Jack? I don't really share my problems with him. I just went to see him when I had the panic attack because I didn't know what it was. I thought I was having a heart attack."

"You didn't mention a panic attack."

"Well, I am not exactly proud of it."

"Anxiety is nothing to be ashamed of, Drew. We all experience it at points in our lives. It manifests itself in different ways for different people. You have several brothers, correct?"

"I do. Six brothers."

"And do you worry about all of them?"
"I do. They all have complications in their lives."

"Have all of them come to talk to you about them?"

"No, not all of them."

"But you still feel obligated to carry those burdens and come up with solutions?"

"Well, yes. They are my brothers." Archer made some notes on a legal pad. "Was that the wrong answer?"

"There are no wrong answers, Drew. I am just making some notes. Tell me about your marriage." Drew smiled broadly.

"It's perfect."

"There are no perfect marriages."

"Well, this one is as close as it gets."

"Okay, how long have you been married?"

"Twenty-six years. But, we have been together almost thirty-one."

"I see. Congratulations. That is quite an accomplishment these days. You have one child together?"

"Yes, my son, Braxton. He is twenty."

"Does he still live at home?"

"He does. He is going to school and working for Shiloh Warner, the local vet." Archer continued to make notes on his pad.

"What are you writing? It makes me nervous."

"I am just writing down some notes, Drew. You don't want me to have to ask you the same questions over and over, right?" Drew sighed.

"So, do you and your wife ever fight?"

"Nope, we never argue."

"And why is that?" Drew pondered the question. He wasn't sure how to answer.

"Do you argue with your brothers?"

"No. I am just not the type to argue I guess."

"Is that because you never disagree or because you feel pressured to be the guy who never argues? Perhaps people come to you with all their problems because they know you will never challenge them?" Again, Drew pondered what the doctor was saying.

"I don't know how to answer that."

"I didn't really expect an answer. It's just something for you to think about."

"I feel like I have a lot to think about," Drew said glumly.

"Introspection is a very healthy exercise."

"I'm not sure I like it."

Archer smiled. "I don't know many people who do. Let's wrap up for today. Are you thinking you might like to continue these sessions?" Drew nodded. "Excellent. Does this time work for you? I think we should chat once a week for now. When you feel like things aren't quite so overwhelming, we can reassess the cadence." The two men stood.

"I'll see you next week. Thank you, Dr. Mangum."

"Archer, please. If you need anything before our next session, please don't hesitate to call."

Drew was lost in thought on his drive home from Watson Grove. If what Archer Mangum was suggesting was true, his whole life was a lie.

The next week was difficult for Drew. Things between him and Angelica were strained as he questioned the beliefs he had about his marriage. He was short with his brothers when they called for advice or just to chat. He avoided calls from both of his parents, and he was having a terrible time concentrating at work.

"I have never seen him like this, Jack," Ange said as she sipped her coffee. She had stopped by his office. "He is angry and unhappy and just in a general funk."

"He has been like that with everyone, Ange. Try not to worry. Sometimes therapy throws you for a loop and you have to do some soul-searching before you come out the other side. He will work through whatever this is and things will go back to normal soon." Jack tried to be reassuring, but he was worried about his brother as well. So worried, in fact, that he had called Archer Mangum the day before to get his take on what was happening with Drew. Archer told Jack the same thing that Jack was telling Ange. Patience and time.

"How did this last week go for you?" Archer asked Drew at the start of their session.

"Not good. I don't know what to believe. As I think about who I am and how I interact with my wife and my family, I am not sure what to think. It's like I don't know who I am anymore."

"This is all normal, Drew. It's quite common when someone starts therapy to feel worse, to be confused about things, and to start to question the major elements in your life. Therapy is a treatment. Just like you might experience side effects from taking medication, there can be side effects from your work here. It's not uncommon for people to experience stress or strains in relationships. I encourage you to continue to do the work even though it's difficult and uncomfortable."

"This just isn't what I expected."

"What were you expecting?"

"I don't know. To come here and talk about things so I could feel better and not have anxiety anymore."

"I wish it were as simple as that, Drew. I would be out of a job which would make me quite happy actually. But, unfortunately, it doesn't work that way. This will be a long, slow journey for you. You will learn a lot about yourself. Some of it you will like and some of it will be painful and upsetting."

Their session continued with Drew talking about the expectations he felt others had of him. When Archer asked what expectations he had for himself, Drew could not easily answer. They ended the session with a list of things for Drew to think about for the following week.

Drew left feeling more overwhelmed than he had since starting to talk to Archer. He drove home, calling in to work and letting them know he wouldn't be coming in. His phone rang. It was Angelica, probably checking in on how his session with Archer went. He let the call go to voice mail. Instead, Drew picked up his phone and dialed Paxton.

"Hey, Drew."

"Pax, question for you. Is there a room at the inn open that I could stay in for a while?"

"Drew, what's going on?"

"I'm just working through some stuff right now and I need to do it alone. Is there a room or not?"

"Yeah. The room upstairs from me is open. I can call Neal and let him know you want it. Have you talked to Ange about this?"

"No, I will. Just call Neal. I am on my way over." Drew hung up. As he pulled in his driveway, it was as if he was at someone else's house. Everything about his life felt so foreign to him. On the way to the bedroom, Drew surveyed the photos, the memories that lined the walls of his home. Once in the bedroom, he pulled a suitcase out of the closet and packed some clothes and toiletries. His phone rang again. It was Jack. Paxton must have called him. Again, he let the call go to voicemail. Drew put his suitcase in the trunk and got in the car. His hands were shaking as he reached for the wheel. Was he leaving his wife? His life? He couldn't answer his own questions. He backed out of the driveway and headed for the Chesterton Inn.

The Pride of a Father

"So, tell me about how this last week went for you, Drew," Archer asked at the start of their session.

"I moved out, if that's any indication of how things are going." Frustration and fear were evident in Drew's voice.

"How do you feel about that?"

"Really? My whole life is in upheaval and I've just told you that there was this major happening and all you can ask is how I feel about it?"

"What reaction were you expecting from me?"

"I don't know, surprise maybe? It feels like a big, scary dramatic step."

"Actually, I'm not surprised. This is all part of the process, Drew. Furthermore, this isn't about me. I have no opinion on what you do or say. I am neutral in that regard. I am just here to listen and to help. Let's talk about why you moved out. As far as I can tell, you are still in love with your wife. So, why did you feel it necessary to leave?"

"Everything I thought was true about myself, my life, my marriage has all been called into question. I don't know what to believe anymore."

"So you felt like you needed to leave to have the space to sort things out?"

"I guess so."

"That doesn't sound so dramatic or scary."

"Tell that to my wife."

"What was her reaction?"

"She's angry with me. I think her feelings are hurt even though I tried to explain that this was about me and not about her at all. She's confused."

"How did you leave things with her?"

"I don't know. Undone, I guess."

"Do you want to bring her to your next session? I would be happy to talk to you both if you think it would be helpful." Drew pondered the suggestion.

"Can I think about it?"

"Of course. It doesn't have to be next week. Anytime you are ready or you think the time is right for her."

Ange relied heavily on her tribe of sisters-in-law as she tried to figure out why Drew had left her. She couldn't come up with any event, any reason for what was happening. It was as if things were fine one minute and broken the next. Communications with Drew were infrequent and uncomfortable when they did occur. Ange was beside herself with worry but trying to put a brave face on for Braxton. Brax was at a loss as to what was going on between his parents. He had never seen his father be anything but steady and even-keeled. He was worried about them both.

Drew continued his introspection, going to work and then back to the inn, locked away trying to figure things out. His sessions with Archer were unsettling even though he was assured progress was being made. It wasn't until Jakob arrived at the inn that evening that his perspective and priorities became clear.

OWEN

The Breakup

Owen intently watched his brothers chatting with each other and with Jack's guests at the retirement party. He felt like he was still the black sheep even though he wasn't there with Scotty. Scotty Donovan was Owen's ex-boyfriend. The two had recently broken up after almost six years together. Owen was suffering but didn't feel like he could share his unhappiness with his family. Being raised in the conservative, military Cooke family had made dealing with questions about his sexual preferences difficult and disclosing that information to his family painful and uncomfortable. His own military service was challenging and his father's unspoken disappointments even more so.

Owen shut off the shower and grabbed his towel, drying his hair and wrapping the bath sheet around his waist. His muscular frame kept in shape by several workouts a week fit well with his chiseled good looks. His dark hair coupled with blue eyes the color of Caribbean waters attracted both women and men easily. His square, rugged jaw adorned with a cleft in his chin just added to his physical appeal. He was almost finished shaving when he heard the doorbell. *It must be a package,* he thought to himself as he continued to shave. The bell rang again. Owen sighed. He dried his face and grabbed a pair of shorts, pulling them on as he headed for the door.

"What are you guys doing here?" Owen asked as he opened the door to Clayton and Blane Schuler, the couple that he and Scotty had done just about everything with. The four were close to inseparable before Owen and Scotty split. Since then, all of them had struggled with how to move forward with their friendship.

"Hey, Owen," Clayton said, "Can we come in?"

"Sure. What's going on?" The three men went into the living room. "Clayton?"

"Sit down, Owen."

"You're freaking me out, guys. What is going on?" Owen demanded as they all three sat down.

"Owen, it's Scotty," Clayton said.

"Yeah, what about him?" Owen replied bitterly.

"The police found his body this morning. They think it was an overdose," Blane said. Owen felt like the world had stopped, like things were moving in slow motion.

"Owen?" Clayton's voice snapped him back to reality.

"But he was clean. Almost seven years," Owen said.

"He started using again after the breakup," Blane replied.

"Why didn't you say anything?"

"He asked us not to," Clayton explained. "We tried to get him back to meetings or into rehab, but he wasn't having it."

"How did you find out?"

"He was staying in one of the apartments in the building we own."

"Did he do this on purpose?" Owen asked, afraid of what the answer might be.

"The police didn't find a note or anything that would indicate it was suicide. They think it was likely accidental." Owen nodded, trying to take in what was happening. He sat silently on the sofa, clutching a throw pillow against his belly.

"Owen, let us call someone. Let us call Gavin." Owen didn't respond.

"Where's your phone?" Blane stood, waiting for his answer.

"Kitchen, I think." Blane went to the kitchen to look for the phone.

"Owen, are you okay?" Clayton asked. Owen was silent. Only a shrug of the shoulders acknowledged that he even heard what was being said. In the kitchen Blane called Gavin and explained the situation.

"I'm on my way. I should be there in twenty minutes," Gavin said as he looked at his calendar and made a note for his secretary so she could reschedule his afternoon. He got in the car and drove towards his brothers apartment. En route, he picked up the phone and dialed Drew.

"Hey, Gavin. What's up?"

"Hey. I am on my way to Owen's. Get this, evidently Scotty overdosed last night. The cops found his body this morning."

"Holy shit, Gavin! How is Owen?"

"I don't know. I haven't talked to him yet, but one of his friends called. I am on my way to his place now."

"Do I need to come too?"

"Sit tight. Let me see how things are with him. I'll call you later."

The next few days were intense. Gavin was staying with Owen, much to Owen's objections. The other Cooke brothers were in constant contact, making Owen feel a bit overwhelmed. Even though he knew they meant well, all he wanted was for everyone to just leave him alone and let him wallow in the abyss of grief he was feeling. Things with Scotty felt so undone, like there was no closure at all, and Owen was struggling. He had been using his vacation time to stay home from work and hadn't left his apartment since Clayton and Blane had arrived to tell him the news. He wasn't eating or sleeping, and Gavin was worried.

Owen had been in touch with Scotty's family, and per his wishes, there was to be no funeral service. Gavin suggested getting some friends together for a memorial service. Owen declined the offer. Gavin then suggested going to Collingswood to spend some time with the family. Again, Owen declined.

The Road to Nowhere

Two weeks had passed since Scotty's death, and Owen was a mess. Gavin had moved back to his own place. Owen went from being a complete recluse, ignoring calls and visitors, to going out every night, drinking way too much, and partaking in meaningless one-night stands. The family was worried. Gavin was so worried, in fact, that he decided to reach out to someone from Owen's past.

Caelan Wessex was Owen's first love. The two met when they were studying at the University of Illinois. The two were very close, but the relationship had ended after four years when Caelan had to return to the United Kingdom. There was much discussion about Owen joining him there, but in the end, it didn't work out. Owen stayed in Chicago and worked as a teacher at the university. It took some doing, but Gavin was finally able to locate a phone number for Caelan Wessex.

"Hello?"

"Caelan?"

"Yes. Who's calling, please?"

"This is Gavin Cooke. I'm not sure if you remember me."

"Owen's brother, the architect. Of course, I remember. Gavin, how are you?"

"I'm good, how about yourself?"

"Fine, thank you. To what do I owe the pleasure of this call?"

Gavin took a deep breath knowing there was no turning back. Owen was going to be very angry. "I am calling about Owen."

"Is everything okay?"

"Yes and no. He's fine. I mean, there hasn't been an accident or a horrible diagnosis or anything like that. But, before we get into what's going on. I was hoping I could ask you a couple of questions."

"Okay, sure. Ask away."

"Well first, are you seeing anyone? Married? In a relationship? I don't want to cause any problems for you, and Owen would never forgive me if my reaching out led to trouble."

Caelan smiled. "I am not seeing anyone, not married, and not in a relationship."

Gavin breathed a sigh of relief.

"Where are you these days? I expected a UK number, but what I dialed is in the states."

"I own a small internet security company, and I live in Alexandria, Virginia, just outside of DC. What about you and Owen? Still in Chicago?"

"Yep. Both of us are still here. I am still with the same architectural firm and Owen is still teaching at the university."

"Okay, so we've gotten the niceties out of the way, and you've determined you aren't going to break up any sort of relationship, so can we cut to the chase and talk about what's going on with Owen."

"Sure. About six month ago, he broke up with Scotty. Did you know about him? I'm not sure how long it has been since you two were in touch."

"Yes, I met him once, maybe a year after they started dating. We had drinks when I came through Chicago on business. I'm sorry to hear they ended things. He seemed like a nice guy."

"A couple of weeks ago, Scotty was found dead. He overdosed on prescription meds."

"Oh, dear God. That's horrible! How is Owen?"

"That's the reason for my call. He is not doing well at all. I am very worried as is the rest of the family. He's drinking and there is a parade of one-night stands. He's pushing everyone away. I don't know what else to do."

"How can I help, Gavin? Name it."

"I think it might help him to see you."

"If you think it will help things then I am on a plane, but what makes you think seeing me will make any difference at all?"

"I have always thought that for Owen, you were the one who got away."

Again, Caelan smiled. "I have always felt the same way. I will get on the next flight out. I will call you when I land."

Gavin hung up from his conversation with Caelan and dialed Jack.

"How are things going up there? How's Owen?"

"Owen is the same, Jack. And I just did something that is either going to make things significantly better or significantly worse."

"Oh boy, what did you do?"

"I called Caelan. He is on his way here."

Jack whistled. "You weren't kidding. I hope it's the right thing."

"Me too. I had to try something."

"Well, keep me posted on how things go."

The Questions of the Future

Owen was lying on the couch, trying to recover from the binge drinking he had taken part in the previous evening when he heard a knock on the door.

"Go away!" He was in no mood to talk to whoever was out there. He knew it wasn't Gavin because his brother had a key and wasn't afraid to use it. Another knock. Owen sighed. He got up and stomped to the door. "Didn't you hear me say go away?" he bellowed as he pulled the door open. Owen's eyes immediately welled up with tears when he saw Caelan Wessex standing at his door.

"Can I come in?" Caelan asked as he pushed his way into Owen's apartment. It was a disaster, which was very unlike Owen's neat-freak tendencies. Caelan set down his bag. "Go, take a shower."

"What are you . . . "

Caelan interrupted. "Go take a shower, Owen. We can talk once you're done." Owen complied, too stunned to argue. Caelan found the box of garbage bags under the sink and went to work gathering up the trash. He loaded the dirty dishes into the dishwasher and wiped down the kitchen counters. When Owen got out of the shower, he found Caelan in his bedroom stripping the bed.

"You don't need to do that," Owen said as he walked into his closet to find something to wear.

"Yeah, I do, Owen. Someone needed to and you aren't the one it seems. Where are the clean sheets?"

"Linen closet in the hall." Caelan found the sheets and pillow cases and went to work on making the bed. Owen dressed in jeans, a t-shirt, and a hooded sweatshirt with the university logo on the front.

"Mind telling me what you are doing here?"

"Why don't you go first and tell me what's going on with you, Owen? This place is a mess, and you're a mess. What's happening here?" Again, Owen's eyes brimmed with tears. His emotions were raw.

"You heard about Scotty?"

"I did. I'm so sorry."

"I'm lost and overwhelmed and not sure how to move forward, Caelan."

"So, I get that. But I don't think living in squalor, boozing it up every night, and sleeping with every guy who crosses your path is your best bet." His words stung, but Owen knew he was right.

"How long are you in town?"

"As long as I need to be. I came specifically to sort you out, Owen. However long it takes."

"Gavin called you?"

"He did."

"He had no right."

"He was worried about you. That's saying a lot, Owen. Gavin is not the type to worry about anyone." Owen sighed. He was exhausted and his head was pounding. "I am going to make you something to eat. Then you are going to get some rest before we talk this through and figure out how to get you out of this destructive cycle."

Too tired to argue, Owen followed Caelan into the kitchen and watched as he found the things he needed for an omelet. Owen didn't realize how hungry he was until he smelled breakfast cooking. Caelan made two plates, handing one to Owen and taking the other to the kitchen table. Owen followed. Caelan's phone rang. "I need to take this, sorry." Owen was able to glean from hearing Caelan's side of the conversation that it was someone he worked with and there was an issue they were going to meet about later today.

"I'm sorry if this took you away from your work."

"Some things are more important that work, Owen. Plus, I can work from anywhere as long as I have an internet connection, so don't worry about it."

"What are you doing these days anyway? Last time I saw you, you were working for that big security company. You hated it."

Caelan chucked. "That's true, I did hate it. I hated it so much that shortly after I started my own company. Now I'm the boss and my employees are probably having dinners with their friends telling them how much of an ass I am."

"I doubt that. But it's great that you are your own boss. I get so tired of the bureaucracy and politics of the university."

"You've been there a long time."

"That I have."

"Speaking of which, when are you supposed to be at work?"

"I haven't been since Scotty . . . " Owen still couldn't say the words out loud. "I have been using my vacation time."

"Do you want to go back?"

"What? You mean quit? I can't afford it."

"You could take a leave of absence. They have a sabbatical program, right?"

"I think they do. I think it's one week for every year of service plus two weeks additional that are unpaid."

"So that would give you twenty-one weeks, nineteen of those as paid time. I think you should do it."

"I will call and see what the options are for sure. I'm quickly running out of vacation time anyway and I'm not ready to go back." The two men ate in silence.

"What if this was my fault, Caelan?"

"You and Scotty weren't together at the time, right? How could it be your fault?"

"Maybe if I would have done things differently, we would have stayed together. I could have stopped him from taking the pills."

"I think that's a bit of a reach, Owen. First, some relationships run their course and they end. It's not because of an event or something one person did; they just end. And, secondly, you weren't responsible for Scotty's sobriety. Only he could make the decisions about whether or not he was going to take the pills. It's my understanding this has been ruled as an accidental overdose and not a suicide, so it's no one's fault. It's just a tragic ending to a bad decision."

Owen watched him intently. He had forgotten how attractive Caelan Wessex was. His spiky light brown hair had a tiny start of gray, and a scruffy hint of a beard framed his mouth. His lips were soft, the top thinner against the bottom which was full and almost pouty. His gray-blue eyes set under thick, full brows were almost steely in nature.

"You need to get some rest, Owen. You look exhausted." Caelan stood and took the plates, rinsing

them in the sink then putting them into the dishwasher.
"I have some work to catch up on. Go take a nap and we
can talk more later." Owen didn't argue. He was
exhausted, and although the food made him feel better,
the headache was still present. He stood to go to the
bedroom.

"Thank you for coming, Caelan." Caelan stepped
towards him, putting his arms tightly around Owen's
shoulders.

"Everything's going to be okay. I promise."

As he went into the bedroom to lay down, Owen's
phone rang. "I should kill you."

Gavin laughed, "You probably should. How are things
going?"

"I seriously can't believe you called him."

"Me either, actually. But you sound better than you
have in a while, so I guess it was the right thing to
do."

"We'll see. I am on strict orders to take a nap, so
I better go. I will call you tonight."

Over the course of the next few days, Owen and
Caelan had several long conversations. They talked about
the past and what had happened between them,. concluding
that the reason they ended was timing more than anything
else. A good amount of time was spent talking about
Owen's relationship with Scotty. While he was in it, Owen
never really paid much attention to the issues, but as he
peeled back the layers in hindsight, he realized that it
wasn't a very healthy coupling. Owen talked to the
university about the sabbatical and was more than
relieved when they were gracious and accommodating about
his request. With the pressure of the job off the table,

he felt like he could focus on working through his issues.

Caelan provided incredible care and support, being gentle and understanding but also honest and stern when necessary. There was a certain level of comfort between the two though Caelan was very careful to keep his distance and not let things move into something other than just a friend supporting a friend.

It was two weeks later when a pressing meeting called Caelan back to Washington, D.C. The two agreed to get back together a couple of weeks later, open-ended on who would travel where or if they would meet somewhere in the middle. There was some discussion about the future and what their relationship could be, but Caelan was insistent that Owen get through what he was feeling now, to get to a healthier and happier place before there was any conversation about where the two of them were going. Caelan desperately wanted to reconcile with Owen. It wasn't until he had seen him a couple of weeks before that he realized just how much regret he had over the two of them splitting up. Only time would tell what might happen between the two.

They were in constant contact through texting, emails, and video calls. Owen, coming out of the fog he was stuck in, spent his days organizing his thoughts and his life, doing a serious purge of his belongings. It felt good to be lighter. He was looking forward to meeting with Caelan the following weekend in Roanoke, Virginia. They had booked an Airbnb in the Blue Ridge Mountains. The plan was set until Owen received the call from Gavin . . .

GAVIN

The Thaw

Gavin sighed as he watched his father dote over Jack. Cord Cooke always doted over Jack, at least in Gavin's mind. Jack was the golden child, the favorite. He was the perfect combination. Every parent would be proud that their child was a doctor. Add to that his successful military career, and Jack was sure to be a favorite.

Gavin thought that perhaps Jack couldn't have been more perfect in the eyes of their father. He had been envious of Jack for years. Jack's life was perfect. Everything had always fallen into place for him. Years ago, Gavin thought he was going to have his own perfect life. He was a gifted athlete in several sports, but baseball was his love. He was the starting pitcher in both high school and college. He had four years of high-school state championships, two national championships at the collegiate level, and a college scholarship attributed to his pitching talents. It was almost certain he would get called up to the major leagues.

That was before his career-ending shoulder injury, before his world came crashing down around him. Gavin was quite handsome, very popular, able to get just about any woman he wanted. He was also somewhat vain, worried that his good looks were fading as he aged. He took steps to prevent that, steps he would be mortified if his brothers knew about: frequent facials, anti-aging products, and an appointment every six weeks with his stylist to cover up any gray hairs. He was used to being the center of attention. He had a bit of a cocky attitude and acted as if he were superior to everyone else. Those behaviors were all connected to his athletic prowess, and when that was gone, his identity was undefined. Now, thirty years after the direction of his life had changed, he still didn't have his arms around who he was, no clue how he fit into his family or the world at large. He was still cocky and could be considered condescending.

Gavin was a successful architect at the Rivershade Architectural Design in Chicago. While he impressed the partners and interfaced well with clients, he was not well-liked by his peers. The reality was, Gavin didn't have any friends. He dated often but was incapable of connecting with someone on an intimate level. His only real friend was his brother Owen; the two of them related because neither felt like they were accepted by the family. Gavin was sure his father was disappointed in him for not being able to pursue the baseball career so the two rarely talked. Cord did not feel that way at all but was not great at opening up and discussing relationship matters with his sons or with anyone.

Cord Cooke was a stoic military man and didn't know how to be anything else. Beverly, the matriarch of the Cooke family, was the peacemaker, trying to smooth things over between the brothers and between Cord and his sons. As a result, when she told her boys things about their father and how he felt, they didn't always believe her as they thought she was just trying to soothe their feelings.

In his own way, Gavin was a bit jealous of each of his brothers: Chance with his wife and kids; Paxton with his climb up in the construction company; Drew, the nice guy everyone loved with his perfect marriage; Jakob, who had built a very successful business from nothing; and

Owen, who was brave and social and funny. All of his brothers had attributes he wished he could emulate, but the anger and bitterness of the hand he was dealt seemed to override the ability to make changes.

Gavin was relieved when the party was over and he could go upstairs away from everyone. His family overwhelmed him at times. Gavin sighed when there was a soft knock at the door. "Yeah?"

"You okay?" It was Owen.

"Yeah, just partied out. Tired of hearing Dad blow Jack's horn. How about you? How are you faring?"

"Okay, I guess. Ready to go home tomorrow, that's for sure."

"Have you heard from him?"

"Scotty? No, I don't expect to. He is already dating other people."

"You okay with that?"

"No, but I can't really do anything about it."

"Come out with me next week. You can be my awesome gay wingman."

"Wow, now that's an offer if I ever heard one," Owen joked. "I'm heading to bed. I'll see you in the morning."

"Night."

The next morning, the Cookes descended on The Tulip Diner, everyone meeting for breakfast before Cord,

Beverly, Gavin, and Owen left for Chicago. They ate, chatted, teased, reminisced. Any outsider would have never seen the cracks in the façade of this seemingly perfect family. Gavin hated these big meals with everyone talking over each other, teasing and laughing. He felt uncomfortable, like an outsider in his own family.

That same week, Gavin held to his word, dragging Owen out with him to his favorite bar. The two handsome brothers had no problem attracting attention from the ladies. They had a few drinks and danced to a few songs before Owen decided to head for home, leaving Gavin with a table of ladies. Gavin ended up leaving with one of the young women, going to her place for more drinks and a one-night stand. Gavin never stayed, never gave the women his number, and was pretty straight forward about telling them not to expect a repeat encounter. Gavin wasn't looking for a relationship. Actually, that wasn't necessarily true. Gavin wasn't capable of a relationship. He would love to be married, to have a successful marriage like Drew or Chance or Pax. He simply wasn't able to let anyone get close.

The next morning, Gavin was in his car driving home from his latest fling. He was in a rush to get to his condo and get changed for a client meeting that he didn't want to be late for. He was distracted, glancing down at his phone to check the time for the meeting when he heard the thud. He slammed on the brakes, unsure of what he had hit. When he got out of the car, he saw the little pink bicycle and a wave of nausea washed over him. He ran around to the front of the car and saw her lying there, not moving. "Please don't be dead," he whispered. He went to her, bent to touch her arm, and heard her moan. "Oh, thank God!" he said as he dialed 911 on his cell phone.

"911. What's your emergency?"

"I just hit a little girl on a bicycle with my car," Gavin said, his voice shaking.

"Is she breathing?"

"Yes, she is moaning."

"What's your location, sir?"

"I am on Front Street heading north, between Spruce and Levine."

"I have dispatched emergency responders and police. They should be there shortly."

"Please hurry." Gavin hung up and called his office, reaching his assistant Judy. He explained that he had been in an accident and needed her to push back everything on his schedule for the day. The ambulance arrived and the paramedics assessed the child for injuries. Thankfully, other than a cut on her leg, a few cuts and scrapes, and a big scare, she was basically unharmed. Gavin was issued a $234 ticket for distracted driving after the ambulance left the scene to take the girl to the hospital. The first responders departed, leaving Gavin shaken in his vehicle. He picked up his phone and dialed.

"Hey, brother. What's up?" Jakob asked. It was unusual for his brother to call on a workday.

"Jakob, I was in an accident."

"When? Are you okay? Are you hurt?" Jakob moved from behind his desk and paced the floor in his office.

"Can I stay with you if I come there?"

"Gavin, you didn't answer my question. Where are you? And, yes, of course you can stay with me."

"I'm fine. No injuries. I'm going to drive down in the next couple of hours. I have a stop to make."

"Are you sure you should be driving? You sound pretty shaken up."

"I'm fine. I will see you later this afternoon."

Gavin drove to the hospital where he presumed the ambulance would have taken the girl. He parked, went inside, and told the emergency room desk attendant his story. She took pity on him as he was obviously distraught and went to find the girl's parents. Gavin waited, pacing, terrified that there would be some complication with the girl's health. A few minutes passed and a tall lanky man in a business suit came through the doors with the woman from the desk. She pointed to Gavin and the man strode over. "Hi, I'm William Bentin," he said, reaching out his hand for a handshake.

"Gavin Cooke," Gavin firmly gripped his hand. "How is she?"

"She's doing well. Nothing serious. They just wanted to check her out to see if there was anything like a concussion. So far, everything is fine. I think she is going to be able to go home in the next couple of hours."

"Oh, thank God! I was so worried. I am so sorry." His eyes were glassy with tears.

"Thank you for stopping by to check on her. She shouldn't have been riding her bike there. We've told her a hundred times to stay in our cul-de-sac, but she is adventurous," he said with a kind smile.

"I'd like to replace her bicycle. It's the least I can do. And, of course, I would like to cover any medical bills."

"That's very generous, but it's really not necessary."

"Please, it would make me feel better."

"Okay, sure," William reluctantly agreed. He could see that Gavin was shaken and feeling terrible about the accident. Gavin gave him his business card with all his information.

"Please call my office and let me know what bike she would like. She should pick out whatever she wants, and please, forward all the medical bills to my office."

"Thanks again for stopping by."

Gavin apologized again as the two men shook hands. He felt better knowing she was going to be okay. He headed for his car and drove to his condo to pack a bag. He just wanted to get away from the city.

On the five-hour drive to Collingswood, Gavin had plenty of time to think. He was shaken by the accident. Not just about the child he could have killed but about his life in general. He wasn't happy with the way things were, but he didn't know how to go about making a change. He desperately wanted a relationship like Drew had with Ange or like Chance had with Waverly. He had always wanted kids, but now that he was fifty, he figured that ship had sailed. Time was marching on and Gavin didn't feel like he had much to show for his life so far. He mulled things over in the quiet of the car. Thankfully, since it was the middle of the day, traffic was light and he made good time.

Gavin drove to Jakob's new apartment. He had recently moved onto the farm of the local vet who happened to be Jack's neighbor both at work and at home. As he pulled in, Jakob came down the stairs to meet him.

"Are you okay? Do we need to go see Jack and have him check you out?"

"I'm fine, Jakob. It was just a minor thing. It was stupid really."

"What happened?"

"I hit a little girl riding her bike because I was looking at my phone."

"Jesus, Gavin! Is she okay?"

"She is, thank God! I stopped by the hospital and met her father before I left to come here."

"And the car? It looks okay. Do you want me to call Martin and have him check it over?" Martin Elvish was the owner of Elvish Motors & Gas.

"Sure. I guess it couldn't hurt. I am probably due for maintenance stuff anyway."

"Did you bring a bag?" Gavin popped the trunk and Jakob grabbed both the overnight bag and the briefcase. "Come on in." They two men trotted up the stairs and into the apartment.

"This is pretty nice, Jakob. How long have you been here?"

"Only about a week. I will say it's better than sleeping on Karl's couch." Gavin chuckled. He had known Karl for as long as Jakob had. Just thinking about sleeping on his couch didn't sound comfortable at all. Karl Arnold was a Bell County deputy sheriff. While he was a great cop, he was a bit of a slob. His apartment looked like a college dorm room with old shabby furniture, pizza boxes, and state-of-the-art television and video-game consoles.

"Are you hungry? We could go grab some lunch if you want," Jakob suggested.

"I'm not hungry, but thanks for the offer. I have some work I need to do. I'm guessing that you have plenty of work to do as well. You don't need to entertain me."

"Okay, man, if you're sure."

"I'm sure." Jakob gave Gavin the wifi password and went to the bedroom to continue working on his own list of tasks.

Gavin responded to emails, reviewed a set of plans and provided his input, then called his boss to let him know he needed to work remotely for the rest of the week. He called his assistant Judy and asked her to set up a conference call with the clients he was supposed to meet with earlier that morning. Jakob came through the living room and into the kitchen for something to drink.

"Jakob, could we keep the accident between the two of us? I don't want everyone making a huge deal out of nothing."

Jakob leaned against the counter and took a drink of juice. "Sure."

Projects Close to Home

Later that afternoon, Jakob introduced Gavin to Shiloh. The two of them seemed to instantly hit it off. They chatted about the sanctuary, the animals, Shiloh's vet practice, and Gavin's two horses. The three of them completed the outside chores together, Gavin asking a hundred questions about the animals and their care. "I am going to head inside and take care of the little guys," Shiloh said.

"I'd like to come with you," Gavin offered.

"Sure! Jakob? Are you joining our critter party?"

"I am going to send over some pictures to a client and change my clothes. You two go ahead and then I will take you both out to dinner." Gavin followed Shiloh inside, meeting the pig, the cat, and the dogs. He and Shiloh chatted about the care for each as she cleaned, fed, and medicated the animals.

"You know, you could turn this in to a real cash cow, I think," Gavin said. "How much land do you have?"

"I have just under three thousand acres."

Gavin whistled. "You could turn this into a major attraction. People could come to visit the animals and volunteer. You could apply for charitable status. You could likely make it self-sustaining."

"That sounds overly ambitious, Gavin."

"Yeah, maybe. It would most definitely be a ton of work."

"Honestly, I feel like I'm in over my head at times. It's been so nice having Jakob here to help." Gavin smiled. He had seen the way his brother lit up when he talked about Shiloh, and now seeing him dote on her, Gavin could tell his brother was quickly falling for the red-haired spitfire. Shiloh finished the last of the care for the smaller animals then they went to find Jakob so they could go to get a bite to eat.

"The Tulip Diner? Or are you all in the mood something more fancy?" Jakob asked as they met in the driveway.

"I'm fine with the diner," Gavin said. Shiloh agreed. The three piled into Jakob's truck and drove downtown.

After dinner and a quick stop off at the clinic so Shiloh could check in on a patient, the three were home and off in three separate directions. Shiloh headed inside to get ready for bed and read a book she was having a hard time putting down. Jakob had some additional design work he wanted to do for a commercial client in Watson Grove. Gavin closed himself in the second bedroom and played around with some ideas for how Somerset Sanctuary could become a self-funded attraction. It had been years since he had been this excited about something. He made notes and drew plans for what the acreage could be used for. He worked late into the night, designing a look and feel for the different outbuildings that would be necessary for the various types of animals. It was a nice change for him to be creative without the confines of a customer's desires and budget limiting the possibilities. He didn't know if he would ever share the ideas with Shiloh or anyone else, but for now, it was a great distraction that kept his mind busy and prevented the continued wallowing related to his unhappy life.

The Road to Reconnection

Gavin spent the long weekend creating and designing, coming up with ideas for the sanctuary. He spent time with Jakob and Shiloh, feeling at ease and more accepted than he had in a long time. Maybe it was the change in Jakob since he had left Delilah. Or maybe it was feeling like Shiloh was a neutral third party that had no background on which to judge him. Either way, he was relaxed and actually enjoying himself. Owen had called several times. He was concerned about his brother and the abrupt trip to Collingswood. Gavin had not told Owen or anyone else about the accident. Only Jakob knew and he was true to his word, not sharing the information with anyone else.

Jack stopped by to drop off some produce that the Wagonners had donated for the animals on Saturday evening. "Gavin! I didn't know you were in town!"

"Hey, Jack! I needed a quick getaway from the city. Jakob has been putting up with me for a few days."

"Is everything okay?" Jack was concerned. Voluntary time with the family wasn't really Gavin's style.

"Everything is good, Jack. I'm fine. Let me help you get this unloaded." The two men made quick work of emptying out the back of Jack's truck, storing the produce in the various refrigerators throughout the property. Shiloh joined them in the driveway, giving Jack a quick squeeze.

"I picked up the produce for the week. I was there getting some groceries anyway."

"Thank you, Jack. It was on my list to do today, so you saved me a trip. And thank you both for unloading everything. Lugging it all to where it's supposed to be is not my favorite thing. Jack, are you joining us for dinner?"

"Well, sure! Thanks, Shiloh." Shiloh went back inside to finish dinner and set a place for Jack. "So, are you going to tell me what's really going on?"

Gavin smiled. His brother did know him pretty well. "There's nothing to tell."

"Gavin, you might as well tell me because if Jakob knows, he will collapse like a house of cards when I pressure him to spill the beans. He stinks at keeping a secret." It was true. Jakob couldn't stand to keep a secret if one of his brothers thought he knew something.

"I had a bit of an accident earlier this week."

"A car accident? Are you all right?" Jack immediately slipped into doctor mode.

"I promise I'm fine, Jack."

"Was it serious?"

"I hit a little girl who was riding her bike. Thankfully, she wasn't seriously injured. I ordered her a new bike and am covering all her medical expenses. It's really not that big of a deal."

"You retreated to Collingswood to hang out with your brother. Seems like a big deal."

"I guess it's a big deal in that it shook me up a bit and forced me to deal with some things. I need to make some changes in my life, Jack. I am not sure how, but I need to. I am not happy with the way things are. Not everyone can have the perfect life like you do where everything just falls into place."

Jack chuckled. "You think my life is perfect where everything falls into place? That's funny, Gavin. I have a failed marriage and an ex-wife that I think I might want back, but I'm not sure. It's not really what I had envisioned. Add to that fifteen years of wasted time with Chance. Yeah, that's perfection right there." Gavin was silent. He had never thought about things from Jack's perspective. He had spent so much time being jealous of him he never considered that his brother might have regrets of his own. "So, what changes do you want to make?"

"I don't know, Jack," Gavin said with a sigh, "something's gotta give."

"Is it the job?"

"Not really, the job is fine. I get bored sometimes, but it's fine. I think it's that there isn't anyone in my life. Other than Owen, I have no friends. I date, but there is no one special. I am really alone."

"I'm not sure how someone who has six brothers, three sisters-in-law, two nieces, and a nephew thinks they are alone."

"I've alienated all of them, Jack. You included. I have spent so much time being pissed off at life that I don't really have relationships with any of you."

"So, change it. It's one of the things I am learning because of the situation with Chance. You can't go back. Just go forward." Gavin contemplated what Jack had said as Jakob joined them.

"What's going on here?"

"Gavin was telling me about his accident."

"Oh, thank God!" Jakob breathed a sigh of relief as Jack and Gavin laughed. "Shiloh says dinner is ready." The three brothers continued to chat as they walked inside the house.

Gavin was surprised at how much he enjoyed himself. He found Shiloh delightful, and he and his brothers spent the evening trading embarrassing stories and good-natured barbs. Shiloh cleared the dishes and tidied up the kitchen then excused herself to care for the inside animals. Gavin, Jack, and Jakob made quick work of the outside chores.

"Let's meet for breakfast in the morning before I head back to Chicago," Gavin suggested.

"Sure. What time?" Jack asked as he got in his truck.

"Ten?"

"Okay, then, see you there." Jack backed out of the driveway and headed down the road for his own farm.

"You and Shiloh should join us."

Jakob smiled. "I'll be there. And, I'll let you invite Shiloh."

"It's obvious you are crazy about her, Jakob. Who could blame you? She's pretty wonderful." Jakob blushed as he turned and walked towards the apartment.

Gavin knocked on the back door and stuck his head in the house, calling out to Shiloh. She came down the hallway wearing pajamas with horses printed all over them, holding a book. Gavin chuckled.

"Breakfast tomorrow morning at the diner at ten?"

"Sure. I'll be there."

"I'm heading out after that. I have to get back to the city."

"You are welcome to stay for as long as you like, Gavin. It's been nice having you here."

"Thanks, but I do need to get back. Sleep well and I will see you in the morning."

"Goodnight." Gavin closed the back door and went to the apartment. He decided to call Paxton, Chance, and Drew to see if they were available for breakfast as well. He figured there was no time like the present to start to take Jack's advice. After a brief chat with each of them, they all agreed to meet in the morning.

Gavin was up early making a cup of coffee when Jakob came through dressed for a run. "Morning," Jakob said as he stretched, "Join me?"

"I haven't run in a long time."

"I can take it easy for you," Jakob teased. It used to be that Gavin was in better shape than all of them.

"Nice. Let me change."

Jakob got a glass of water and took some vitamins as he waited for his brother. He was enjoying spending the time with Gavin. It had been years since the two of them had spent any length of time together. Jakob had allowed Delilah to limit his time with his family. Gavin joined him in the kitchen, ready to go.

They turned right out of Shiloh's farm away from town on Bridgeway Trace, running in silence, both lost in their own thoughts.

"Pax, Chance, and Drew are coming to breakfast," Gavin said.

"Oh, a Cooke family reunion. What's going on with you, Gavin? Not that I am complaining, but a big family breakfast would have sent you running for the hills a few weeks ago."

"I know. I think the accident has put some things into focus. I don't want to be pissed and unhappy anymore. Strange how it takes a potentially catastrophic event to make you change."

"Tell me about it. I'm not sure I ever would have gotten out of my horrible marriage had I not caught her in bed with someone else. My life is so much less stressful now."

"And you and Shiloh are going to be a thing?" Gavin poked at his brother.

"I'm not so sure about that. I'd like for us to be a thing, but she is a pretty stubborn and independent woman. We'll have to see if I can get her to open up. What about you? Are you seeing anyone?"

"No, no one special. I think I might like being in a relationship, finding the right woman, settling down like Pax or Chance or Drew."

"Everyone wants to settle down like Drew and Ange. You need to set your sights lower than that. Not everyone gets to have the perfect union."

"Do you think it's really as perfect as it seems?"

"I don't know. Guess I never really thought about it. I kind of like thinking it is. Gives me an aspirational goal." Gavin smiled. They made the turn for home and jogged along in silence once again. When they got back to the farm, Shiloh was just about to start on the outside chores.

"I got this, Shiloh. Go, relax, get ready for breakfast," Jakob said.

"Jakob . . . "

"No argument. Just go." He pointed towards her house. She turned and walked up her back porch stairs and into the house. "See? Stubborn," Jakob said to Gavin.

"Want a hand?"

"Sure." The two made quick work of caring for the animals and getting them situated before going upstairs to shower and get ready for breakfast. Gavin packed his bag, feeling a bit sad at the thought of going back to the city, back to his lonely life.

At the restaurant it was a loud, raucous Cooke breakfast. Chance and Waverly were there. The girls were busy as seventeen-year-olds tend to be. Drew, Ange, and Braxton were there as were Pax and Bits. Gavin reveled in the warmth of his family. Had it always been this way? Had he just been unwilling to accept it? He watched as they chatted and teased and enjoyed being together. How had he missed this for all these years?

After breakfast, Jakob and Shiloh dropped him off at Elvish Motors & Gas so he could pick up his car. "Thanks for letting me stay, Jakob."

"Any time, Gavin. You're welcome here any time." The two shared a handshake and then a one-armed embrace.

"Come back for a visit soon," Shiloh said softly as the two shared a hug.

"I will, Shiloh. Thanks for everything." Gavin felt an overwhelming sadness as he went inside to pay Martin Elvish and get his car. He watched as Jakob and Shiloh pulled away, wondering what the future had in store for them. He hoped good things. His brother deserved an incredible woman like Shiloh. He was lost in thought as he drove through the countryside on his way home.

The next few weeks were ones of reconnection. He had dinner with Owen a couple of times and made a surprise visit to his parents, who lived about forty-five minutes south of Chicago. Things were still strained between Gavin and his father, but for the first time in years, he was genuinely interested in trying to make it better. There were weekly calls between Gavin and his brothers, and he looked forward to catching up with each of them and what was happening in their lives.

He had thrown himself into his job with renewed energy and was enjoying watching the progress unfold on the gallery project. He invited two of his architect colleagues for drinks after work, which was unheard of. The biggest change? He was now dating. He had gone out with two women, neither of whom he really wanted to see again, but his approach was different. Gavin was holding off on taking them to bed and trying to get to know them. He desperately wanted to connect. While these two women were not the spark he was after, he was happy that he was on a different path than he had been before. He was coming out of his funk and was more positive than he had been in years.

It was a Friday night and Gavin was on a date with an attractive woman named Leona. The two were at dinner when Gavin got the call from Jakob . . .

JAKOB

The Past is the Past

Jakob was excited to have his older brother back in town. He and Jack had always been close, and Jakob had always admired him. There were eight years between them. This party was really the first social event Jakob had been to since the breakup of his marriage almost six months ago. Jakob had left his wife Delilah after finding her in bed with another man. As things further imploded around him, it came out that this was not her first affair. In fact, she had been cheating on him since before they married. The reality was, they never should have married. They spent nine very unhappy years married and had dated for seven years prior to that.

Since leaving, Jakob had been staying with his best friend Karl Arnold, a deputy sheriff for Bell County. It was nice to be with his family without the tension that Delilah caused. Over the years, she had done what she could to keep Jakob from spending time with his brothers or his parents. She hated the Cookes and they felt the same about her. His family was saddened by how much Jakob had changed over the years. Jack introduced Shiloh Warner to him and his brothers, and Jakob was smitten. With her short dark auburn hair, gray-blue eyes, and perfect creamy alabaster skin, she was the most beautiful woman he had ever laid eyes on. He couldn't take his eyes off of her. After Shiloh left the party, Jakob took a ribbing from his brothers about his new crush.

In the few days since Jack's retirement party, Jakob had been having a difficult time getting Shiloh Warner out of his thoughts. He was trying to convince himself it was too soon to be interested in a woman, but the truth was, things had been over with Delilah long before the formal demise of his marriage.

Jakob stopped by The Tulip Diner to pick up lunch for himself, Jack, and Shiloh. He was desperate for an excuse to see her. He drove the short distance to Jack's office. "Hey, I brought lunch," he said as he came through the door.

"I see that. But you brought lunch for three," Jack said.

"I thought Shiloh might want something," Jakob said, trying to be casual. Jack raised an eyebrow and stifled a grin.

"That was nice," he said, "Actually, I was going to call you. I had a thought related to Shiloh."

"Not sure what that means, but okay," Jakob said.

"You need a place of your own. Guessing the roommate situation is fine for now but not a permanent living arrangement. Shiloh has an apartment above the barn and I have seen how hard she works to take care of the sanctuary. You two should work out an arrangement so you can move into your own place and she can get the help that she would never admit to needing."

"I like it. Will she go for it?"

"That I'm not sure about. But, it's worth a try. Plus, you can butter her up with lunch. Go invite her here so we can eat."

Jakob went next door to Shiloh's office, trying not to be nervous. "Hey," he said as she came around the corner into the lobby after hearing the bell on the door.

"Jakob! Hi!" she said. He was happy she remembered him.

"Why don't you come next door? I brought lunch," he said, stuffing his hands in his pockets.

"You brought lunch for me?"

"And for Jack," he said turning and opening the door. Come on," Jakob said as he held the door open for her.

Shiloh glanced at her calendar. She had two hours before her next appointment. She picked up her phone and her keys and followed him out, pausing to lock the door. They walked into Jack's office where he had set out the food.

"Hey, Shiloh," Jack said.

"Hey, Jack! It's nice to see you," Shiloh said as she sat in the chair Jack had pulled away from the desk.

The three settled in and ate their lunch, chatting about nothing of consequence. "Shiloh, I wanted to run something by you," Jack said.

"Sure, what's up?" she asked, crunching a chip.

"I don't know if you heard about Jakob's recent breakup from the disaster we call Delilah."

"Sitting right here . . . " Jakob said sourly.

"I hadn't heard. I'm sorry, Jakob," she said.

"Don't be. It was for the best," Jakob said.

"Anyway," Jack continued, "I have noticed how hard you are working, Shiloh, to take care of the sanctuary.

And I know that while Jakob is reliving his teen years having a slumber party with his BFF Karl, he really needs his own place. I was thinking that maybe he could take the apartment above the barn and help out around the sanctuary in exchange for rent."

Shiloh took a long drink of iced tea through her straw as she contemplated what Jack had suggested. Her eyes shifted to Jakob, who was staring into his plate, holding his breath in anticipation of an answer.

"I could use the help," she said, surprising both Jack and Jakob. "Okay, sure," she said, surprising herself. She wiped her fingers on her napkin and picked up her keys, finding the one for the apartment and removing it from the ring. She handed the key to Jakob. "It's been empty for a long time. It probably needs a good cleaning before you move in."

"No problem. Thank you, Shiloh," Jakob said.

"You might want to wait to see what you have signed yourself up for before you thank me," she said with a grin. Jakob smiled. They finished their lunch and headed back to work. Jack needed to see a patient, Shiloh walked back to the clinic to prepare for her next appointment, and Jakob drove to his next landscaping customer.

Jakob owned a landscaping company called Greener Pastures. He had mowed lawns out of desperation after he left the military and flunked out of his first semester of college. Over the years, he had turned it into a prospering business with several teams in Collingsworth and the two neighboring towns of Watson Grove and Barber, a fleet of vehicles and equipment, and hundreds of clients. His primary focus was landscape design these days, but he wasn't afraid to roll up his sleeves and get dirty. He pulled up in front of the house of his next landscaping project and got out to take some photos, finding it difficult to concentrate.

Shiloh was having a tough time concentrating as well but for a different reason. She was kicking herself for agreeing to let Jakob move in. She didn't need help. She was an independent woman, and she certainly didn't need some man telling her how things should be done. *It was a moment of weakness,* she told herself. She sighed and waited for her patient to arrive, an elderly cat who needed his annual checkup.

It was around 7:00 p.m. when Shiloh heard a vehicle pull up in the drive. She had just finished getting the livestock settled for the evening and was on her way to the coop she had for the chickens and turkeys. "Hey, Shiloh," Jakob said as he got out of the truck.

"Hi!" she said, shifting the bag of feed from one hip to the other. Jakob took the bag from her and effortlessly put it over his shoulder.

"This is my friend Karl Arnold. Have you two met?"

"I don't think so. Hey, Karl, it's nice to meet you," she said.

"We wanted to look at the apartment if that's okay? But first, why don't you let us give you a hand with some chores?" Jakob asked.

"Jakob, the apartment is yours. You can come and go any time you like," Shiloh said, "and it's not necessary for you two to help. But thank you."

"Shiloh, if you are going to let me live here without paying rent, that means you are going to have to let me do my fair share around here to earn my keep." Shiloh sighed. "Now, tell me where this bag goes."

"I was heading to the coop to put the birds away for the evening."

"Lead the way."

They walked to the coop, struggled to get everyone to cooperate, and finally got the flock comprised of six chickens, two roosters, four turkeys, and seven ducks settled and fed. "What's next?" he asked.

"Dogs and then cats," Shiloh replied as she walked towards a smaller outbuilding. It was divided in half. One side was set up with cat trees, cat beds, toys, food, water, and litter boxes; the other side had dog beds, old comfy chairs and an old sofa, food, and water. "There are five dogs that need to come in then the dog door needs to be blocked so they can't get out and nothing can get in," she said. Jakob and Karl brought the dogs in, giving each some attention. Jakob used the wood slat to close off the dog door and made sure the food and water dishes were full.

Shiloh moved to the other side of the building to make sure the cat boxes were clean and that the feeders and water bowls were full. She did a head count to make sure all eight of the outdoor kitties were accounted for and blocked the cat door.

"Who's left?" Jakob asked as they stepped outside.

"I just need to medicate Aloysius, my old guy. You don't need to help with that."

"Is he a horse? How old?"

"He's twenty-seven."

"Wow! I'd love to meet him."

"Sure, but he is not as social as he used to be. He's old and a bit under the weather," she warned. Jakob followed her into the barn as Karl stepped outside to take an incoming call. Shiloh stopped in the tack room to pick up the syringe of medication and then strolled to the first stall. "Hey, boy," she said softly as she opened the stall door. Jakob followed her in. Aloysius was towards the back of the stall. As soon as he saw Jakob, he came forward, ears at attention, sniffing and nuzzling at his arm.

"Hi there," Jakob said, letting Aloysius smell his hand before rubbing the horse's nose and face. "It's nice to meet you, big guy." Shiloh was shocked. This was the most engaged she had seen the horse in weeks. "Are you going to let your mom give you some medicine?" Jakob asked as he scratched behind his ears. Aloysius snorted in response. Shiloh gave him the injection in his flank, tenderly rubbing the injection site when she was done.

"There you go, sweetheart. All done," she cooed at him. "I can't believe how alert he is. And how much he likes you. He's not usually that friendly with new people," she told Jakob as they left the stall.

"I'm hard not to like," he said with a grin. Shiloh laughed.

"Are you done with chores?" She nodded as they went outside. "It's dark out here, Shiloh," he said. She stepped back into the barn and turned on the switch. "I could swap out the lights, so they come on automatically when it gets dark," he suggested.

"That would be nice."

"I'll try to get it done this week."

She smiled. "There's no rush, Jakob. You go check out the apartment. I need to head inside and take care of the indoor gang," she said as she walked towards the house. "It was nice to meet you, Karl," she called over her shoulder. Karl waved as he wrapped up his phone call.

The two men bounded up the staircase leading to the apartment over the barn. Jakob unlocked the door and felt around for a light switch. When he found it and flipped the lights on, he couldn't believe his eyes. "Dude, this is a nice apartment!" Karl said. The front door opened facing a bright large kitchen and living area. The space was filled with windows, and in the living room, a sliding glass door opened onto a large wraparound deck. There was a small laundry room and pantry off the kitchen. A hallway led to the main bathroom, guest bedroom, master bedroom, and master bath. The rooms were all large and open, and the closets were huge. Jakob couldn't believe his luck. It was a bit dusty in the apartment, but running the vacuum cleaner and wiping down the surfaces was all that needed to be done before he could move in.

Jakob knocked softly on Shiloh's front door. She answered, and he saw the face of a chocolate-brown pig peeking around her legs. Jakob dropped to his knees, introducing himself to the pig. "Hey, buddy!"

"He's not very friendly with strangers, Jakob. He might nip at you."

"Come here, piggy," he motioned to the pig. "What's his name?"

"Presley," she said, stepping to the side so the two were face to face. The pig cautiously moved towards Jakob, curious but unsure.

"Come on, Presley," he said. "Come say hi!" The pig moved closer and Jakob held out his hand for him to smell. Shiloh cringed, envisioning the pig biting into one of Jakob's fingers. Presley stepped closer, and Jakob slowly moved his hands to pet his head and scratch behind his ears. "You are a handsome guy!" Jakob said, his hands moving down the pig's back. Much to her surprise, the pig flopped over on his side, offering his belly to Jakob for a scratch or two. Jakob obliged as he laughed. "He's really cool, Shiloh."

"You are like the animal whisperer. How is it that my cranky critters seem to think you are a good guy?"

"Maybe because I am a good guy," he said as he stood. "I just wanted to let you know we were heading out. The apartment is perfect. Thanks again for letting me move in."

"Have a good night, Jakob."

"You too. See you around, Presley," he said as he turned and walked to the truck.

"You were a very nice boy, Presley," she said as she locked the door and turned off the lights. "Let's go to bed."

Shiloh went home the following evening after a busy day at the clinic. She would have to go back to the office before bed to give a couple of her surgery patients an evening dose of medication. As she pulled in the drive, she found Jakob on a ladder installing the sensor that would make the lights come on automatically. "You didn't have to do this, Jakob," she said.

"My afternoon was free, so I thought I would take some things over to the apartment and tackle the lighting project. This is the last one."

Shiloh smiled. "Thank you."

"You don't need to thank me, Shiloh."

"I need to do some chores."

"I did the dogs, cats, and birds already. I wasn't sure what you did with the livestock, but if you show me, I will know and can help out with that as well."

"Wow! Really, Jakob, that was above and beyond." He stepped off the ladder and folded it up, leaning it against the barn. Shiloh showed him the evening routine of putting the livestock into the barn and feeding them.

"I can't believe you have been doing all this by yourself," he said when they were finished. "I picked up dinner. Do you want to come upstairs and eat?"

Shiloh didn't know what to say. He had done more for her in one afternoon that anyone had done in years. She nodded, not able to find any words.

They went up the stairs and Jakob opened the door for her. The apartment was sparkling clean. He had moved in a sofa, chair, and coffee table along with a kitchen table and chairs. "I've never seen any furniture in here. It's been empty since I bought the place."

"Well, I don't have much. I left pretty much everything behind. I wanted a clean start," he said as he pulled the food out of the bag. "I hope that Chinese is okay?"

"It's great, but you don't need to feed me."

Jakob smiled as he pulled out paper plates. "Beer?" Shiloh nodded.

They chatted as they ate then put the leftovers in the fridge and gathered up the garbage. "I should go," she said. "I need to do a clean-out of the inside critters and then head back to the clinic to check on my surgery patients and give them meds before bed."

"Can I help?" he asked, not wanting the evening with her to end. He was surprised at how much he was enjoying spending time with her.

"You don't need to do that. You have done so much already," she protested.

"Come on. It will go twice as fast with both of us working on it," he said as he walked towards the door. They went outside and all the outdoor lights came on. Shiloh smiled.

They went in the back door where they were greeted by Presley, who seemed quite happy to see Jakob again. She introduced him to Penelope, the calico cat who was snoozing on the back of the sofa. "I need to let the dogs out of the kitchen and put them in the front yard, so they can eat and go potty without the pig 'helping' them," she said. Jakob went to the kitchen door. It was a Dutch door with the bottom half keeping the dogs and pig separated and the top half open so he could see in. "The black one is Maggie and the yellow one is Track," she called from the other room.

"Hey guys! You want to go outside and go potty and get some dinner?" he asked as the dogs wagged their tails at him. He opened the door and let the dogs out into the fenced area as Shiloh joined them with full food bowls.

They went back inside and down the hallway to a bedroom that had been converted into small pet central. Shiloh picked up the clipboard and went through the checklist of chores for the day. "Okay, we need to clear out the cage materials for the ferrets and change out their litter boxes, clean out the frog aquarium, clean out the sugar glider cage and litter boxes, clear out the guinea pig cage and scoop the cat box. Then we can feed and medicate everyone."

"Tell me where to start."

"You can take the ferrets. The brown one is Pip, and the white one is Amelia. Dump, rinse, dry, and refill the two litter boxes in their cage, clear out and replace the fluffy paper in the bottom level, and make sure they have fresh water and plenty of food in their feeder."

"Got it," he said. Shiloh cleaned the sugar glider area doing many of the same tasks as were needed for the ferrets. She smiled as she heard Jakob chatting with the ferrets and picking them up to pet them and give them kisses.

"I'll do the guinea pigs and you do the frog?" he suggested. She nodded and tidied the frog's area, finishing before him then scooping Penelope's litter box. She went through her list of medications and administered the required ones to each critter, telling them how much she loved them. Jakob smiled as he watched her.

"All done!" she said. "Thank you so much. That went very fast. I dread clean-out days!" She called for Presley, who came down the hall and went into her bedroom. She told him goodnight and watched him go to his bed and lay down. She closed the door. He followed her to the front door as she let the dogs in. They found spots on the sofa in the sun room which they declared as theirs and went to bed.

"Can I drive you to the clinic?" he offered.

"You don't need to do that, Jakob. You have gone out of your way so much tonight."

"I know I don't need to, Shiloh, but I would like to. I know we live in a sleepy little town, but I don't like the idea of you going by yourself at night," he said. "Come on. Let's go." She picked up her keys and bag and follow him out to his truck. They were quiet on the fifteen-minute drive. He went inside with her once they arrived.

"There are two patients I need to check, both dogs, both had surgery today. I just need to do a quick bandage change and give them each a dose of antibiotics and pain meds. It shouldn't take me more than ten minutes or so."

"Take your time. Do what you need to do," he said, sitting down in the lobby.

Shiloh cared for her patients, updated the charts, and made sure they were comfortable and settled for the night. "All done," she said as she joined him in the lobby.

"Everyone doing okay?"

"They are good. Thank you for coming with me." She locked up and they got in the truck. On their way home, they chatted about Shiloh's veterinary career. Her love for animals had her volunteering at shelters ever since she had been in high school. She had attended vet school at Tufts University in Massachusetts and worked for a large veterinary office for a few years before striking out on her own.

He parked in the driveway. "Thank you so much, Jakob. I don't even know what to say. You've done so much to help tonight."

"You don't need to thank me, Shiloh. I enjoyed myself."

They said their goodnights and went in opposite directions to their respective homes.

The next few days had the two of them crossing paths but not really seeing much of each other. Shiloh would find that the bulk of her chores outside were done if Jakob arrived home before her. She hated to admit it, but it was a relief to have someone helping out.

Shiloh woke early on Saturday morning then checked on the inside animals, let the dogs out front into their area, and let Presley out back into his large fenced area to graze. She made herself a cup of tea and a slice of toast and then changed into a pair of shorts, a t-shirt, and some work boots. She stopped by the coop and opened the door for the birds, giving them access to their outdoor space. Then she opened the dog and cat doors for the outside bunch and made sure they had plenty of food and water then went to the barn to turn the livestock out. She went to the tack room to tidy up and do an inventory so she could place an order with the feed store on Monday. She cleaned and organized and swept and then took note of the supplies she needed. She stretched to reach for a supplement on a high shelf, muttering to herself that she needed to be six inches taller. She gasped as she felt his hand on her lower back as he reached over her, easily grabbing the item she was struggling to get. "Sorry, didn't mean to make you jump," he said, handing her the jar. "Good morning, by the way."

"Good morning. Did I wake you?" she asked.

"Oh no, I have been up for a while. I just got back from a run. I have some plants and planters in the back of the truck left over from a job this week. I thought I might do some landscaping around here if that's okay."

"That would be lovely. Will you let me pay for the materials?"

"No, Shiloh. It's part of our deal for you letting me stay here. Do you need my help with anything before I start arranging the plants?" She shook her head. "Okay then. I will catch up with you later this morning." Shiloh watched as he walked away from her, pushing thoughts of how handsome he was out of her head. His thick brown hair with just the slightest waviness, his strong brow, his warm smile, and his eyes. Those blue-gray eyes, like the clearing sky after a spring rainstorm, mostly a soft gray with flecks of bright sky blue.

The loud noise from Jakob slamming the tailgate of his truck brought her back to reality. She went to the equipment shed and got on the tractor. Mowing was the next chore on her list. Jakob smiled as he watched her drive out into the pasture, turn on the bush hog, and start the mowing process.

Jakob spent the next several hours filling pots and flower boxes with beautiful combinations of flowers and greenery. He lined the railing of his deck as well as the front and back railings of Shiloh's porch with flower boxes. He installed hooks on Shiloh's front porch and hung overflowing baskets of flowers and ferns. He pulled sparse rock out of old beds, lined the beds with weed barrier, replaced the rock, and added a new flowerbed around the porch of Shiloh's house. He created a few new beds with rocks, bushes, and flowers in several spots along the driveway and near the outbuildings. He noticed a step on the back porch with a wobbly riser. After saying hello to Presley and giving him a slice of the apple he was eating, he got in the truck to make a quick run to the hardware store to get supplies to make the repair.

Shiloh completed her mowing chores and put the tractor back into the shed. She took in a sharp breath when she saw the amount of work Jakob had done in such a short time. The beds and planters looked beautiful. Her eyes welled up with tears, which was very unusual. She prided herself on not being emotional. "What do you think, Presley?" she asked as she walked by his pen. "He's a pretty nice guy, isn't he?" Shiloh went inside to finish the list for the feed store order. It wasn't long before she heard hammering and went outside to see what the noise was about. She shook her head in disbelief when she found Jakob repairing her step. "Jakob . . . "

"Don't start, Shiloh. The step was wobbly, and the wood was rotting. It needed to be repaired. Do you have any leftover paint from when they did the porch floor?"

"I will check the garage. Do you want something to drink?" she asked.

"Sure, that would be great."

Shiloh went to the garage and found the can of paint he needed as well as a small brush. She stopped in the kitchen on her way through and poured him a glass of lemonade. "Here you go."

"Ah, perfect. Thank you," he said, taking the glass and drinking about half the contents in one go. "That hits the spot." He picked up the paint can, giving it a vigorous shake and used a tool on his key ring to pry the lid open then quickly coated the new wood with the paint. "All fixed," he said, handing the brush to Shiloh and putting the lid back on the can.

Shiloh wasn't used to someone helping her or being kind to her. Her parents were killed in a traffic accident when she was six, so she spent her youth bouncing from foster home to foster home. Despite the adversity, she was an exceptional student and went through undergraduate and veterinary school on scholarships. Because of her trust issues, she wasn't great at relationships. She didn't make close friends and didn't want a romantic relationship after having broken free of an abusive boyfriend years ago. Having Jakob willingly and consistently help her made Shiloh feel both uncomfortable and vulnerable.

The next few days found the two clashing a bit as Shiloh resisted Jakob's help and he kept pushing forward, determined to make her let him do what needed to be done. She was amazed at his willingness to identify a problem and solve it. Sometimes she found things fixed after the fact. But, his "just do it" attitude made her feel like she was losing control; this manifested itself in frustration and sometimes anger directed at him.

"I don't need your help, Jakob!" she almost spat the words at him as he tried to get her to let him look at a piece of equipment that wasn't working. He felt like they had had this conversation a hundred times.

"I get it, Shiloh. You don't need my help. But letting me help you, wanting me to help you doesn't make you any less independent or capable," he said in an even tone, trying not to show her how much she got to him. "Last time I checked, you are not a mechanic and you shouldn't be trying to wrestle an eight-hundred-pound piece of farming equipment by yourself. I'm not a mechanic either, but I do have a full fleet of equipment and could at least take a look and see if it is something I know how to fix."

"Fine," she surrendered, turning to walk away, feeling flustered and frustrated. She felt his hand reach for hers, grasping her wrist.

"Hey, I don't want to fight with you," he said as he pulled her towards him, his arms encircling her shoulders. She pressed her forehead against his broad chest. "Don't be angry, Shiloh." She sighed and stepped away from his embrace.

"I'm not. Do you need me for this?" she asked, her voice still tense but for a very different reason than Jakob thought. He shook his head no. She walked away from him, closing the barn door behind her. Shiloh's mind was racing, her heart pounding. For the first time in years, she felt desire for someone and it terrified her. Jakob found the issue with the equipment. It was an easy fix. He finished and put away his tools, resisting the urge to find her in the barn and instead, taking the stairs to his apartment.

Jakob came home from work the following day to a care package by his front door. He picked up the box and carried it inside. There was a note inside that read:

Peace offering. I'm sorry.

Thanks for all you do and thanks for fixing the baler.

xo S

P.S. – off to deliver baby goats at the Sanders' place

He smiled as he set the card aside and looked to see what was in the box. A loaf of homemade bread, still warm, was wrapped in a red dish towel. He must have just missed her. There was also shepherd's pie with a sticky note with heating instructions, a tin full of chocolate chip cookies, and a six pack of beer. He put the beer in the fridge, opened the tin of cookies, picked up his phone and dialed her number.

"Hello?"

"You know how to butter a guy up," he said as he bit into a cookie.

"I'm so sorry about yesterday, Jakob," she said. He heard a goat bleating in the background.

"We're all good, Shiloh. The care package was unnecessary, but damn, those cookies are amazing. Any babies yet?"

"Not yet. And, I am glad you like the cookies."

"I'm going out to take care of the outside guys. Do you want me to do the inside guys as well?" he asked. Shiloh smiled.

"That would be great. I don't know how late I will be."

"Okay, where is the key?"

"No key. It's unlocked."

"What do you mean it's unlocked? Do you always leave your place unlocked?"

"Most of the time. Why?"

"Shiloh, that's dangerous. Promise me you will start locking your doors," he insisted.

"Okay, okay, I promise," she said "Hey, I gotta go, I think it might be showtime over here."

"Okay. I'll see you tomorrow."

"Goodnight, Jakob."

"Oh, hey, before you go, there is a big family dinner at Jack's place tomorrow. I was hoping you would want to come with me. Jack specifically asked me to include you."

"That sounds lovely. Thanks for the invite. I will see you tomorrow."

"Goodnight," he said with a huge smile on his face, a result of her accepting his offer for dinner.

On the Road to New Beginnings

It had been three weeks since Jakob moved into the apartment. He had finally gone to the post office to put in a change of address a few days before, and when Shiloh got home that evening, the mailbox was full of mail for him. She went inside and dropped her bag, her keys, and her own mail. She went out the back door and up his steps. "Mail call!" she said as he opened the door.

"Oh, ugh. That's a big pile. Sorry," he said.

"Why exactly are you apologizing for getting mail?" she asked with a grin.

Jakob smiled as he thumbed through the pile, stepping aside so Shiloh could come in. They walked to the living room. "Hey, I have these awesome cookies . . . " Shiloh laughed. He set the pile of mail on the table but held onto a large manila envelope. "Ever feel like a complete and total failure?"

"Wow, where did that come from? And, yes, I feel like a total failure on some level pretty much every day. But I thought that was just a me thing," she said. He opened the envelope and pulled out the documents.

"My divorce papers," he said, tossing the documents on the table.

"I'm so sorry, Jakob."

"Wait, what do you mean you feel like a failure every day? Are you serious?" he stepped towards her, taking her hands in his. "You don't have any reason to feel like a failure, Shiloh." She looked at her hands in his.

"How did this get to be about me?" she said, trying desperately to change the subject. He tipped her chin with his finger, bringing her gaze to meet his.

"You don't understand how remarkable you are," he said. Shiloh stepped back, flustered.

"I should go," she said. "I need to get the inside critters done and head back to the clinic."

"I'll do the outside guys and then we can go together," Jakob said firmly, not giving her an option to go by herself. "I will meet you at the truck in an hour."

Shiloh nodded, making a beeline for the door. She hated how rattled he made her feel. Jakob sighed as he watched her leave. A failed marriage and now feelings developing for a complicated, stubborn woman. The two finished their respective chores and drove to the clinic where Shiloh medicated her surgery patient, a cat who had been neutered earlier that day. "Did you eat?" Jakob asked as they took off down Main Street, heading towards home.

"I did, thank you. I had a sandwich." She just wanted to get home and away from the feelings she was trying so desperately to ignore. Jakob sighed. He knew she was pushing him away, but he didn't know why.

Karl joined him at the small table at The Tulip Diner. "Hey, sorry I'm late."

"No worries. How are things?"

"Good. I had a date last night."

"Oh, yeah? Do tell. Was it with Laney?" Laney Albertson went to high school with Jakob and Karl. She had married young and moved to Lexington for several years, only to divorce and move with her children back to Collingswood. Karl had had a major crush on her in high school, but they ran in very different crowds. He had been trying to get up the courage to ask her out for months.

Karl smiled, "Yes, it was with Laney. I think I like this girl, Jakob. What about you? How are things going with Shiloh?" Jakob stifled a smile.

"She's stubborn and infuriating, and I think I might be falling in love with her."

"It's only been a month, Jakob. You're not even divorced yet. Are you are ready to jump back in the fire this soon?"

"Really, it's not that soon. And, for the record, I am divorced. I got the papers yesterday. Look, my marriage was a farce. I haven't felt much but contempt for Delilah for a long time. It's different with Shiloh. There is an attraction for sure, but there's something else. I don't know how to describe it. She's hiding from something, living behind walls, and I don't know why. I don't know if I can break through those barriers."

"You make me feel like a dick. I'm trying to figure out how to get laid and you are trying to 'break through barriers' because you think you might be in love."

Jakob laughed. "There might be something to be said for not making things so heavy and complicated. You know me though, I am a one-woman kind of guy. Nothing would make me happier than to settle down in a happy marriage."

They ordered and ate. Shortly after they finished eating, Karl got a call to respond to a fender bender a few blocks over. Jakob decided to visit the nursery and ended up purchasing four large pots along with bags of soil, plants, and flowers to fill them. He drove to the building that Jack and Shiloh shared, parking in the back alley. He pulled the supplies out of the back of his truck, placing the huge ceramic pots on the wheeled stands. He filled each with some gravel for drainage and then soil. For Jack's office he went with aloe vera, kalanchoe, bromeliad, and foliage with greens and bronzes in a dark green pot.

"Hey," Jakob said as he wheeled the pot through Jack's office.

Jack looked up from his computer. "Um, hey . . . " Jakob pushed the pot into the lobby, moving the loveseat out of the way so he could place the pot in front of the window. "Just put that anywhere," Jack said from behind the lobby desk. "What's going on, Jakob?"

"Nothing. Just trying to brighten up the place."

"I see. Are you trying to brighten up Shiloh's office as well?" Jack asked him, eyebrow arched, a mischievous grin on his face.

"Shut up, Jack."

"Hey, suits me fine. I get to reap the benefits of all these gestures you keep doing to impress her." Jack enjoyed teasing him. He wanted things to work out for Jakob. Delilah and their toxic relationship had taken a deep emotional toll on his brother. Jack was quite fond of Shiloh and he thought the two of them together would be good for both of them.

Jakob walked back through Jack's clinic to the alley to start on the pots for Shiloh's office. He put together two pots for the lobby with pale greens and pale pinks. A third pot bursting with a variety of white blooms was for her office. He went around to the front of the building and opened the door to the lobby. Shiloh poked her head in to see who was there after hearing the buzzer from the door. "Hi there," he said.

"Hi! To what do I owe this pleasure?"

"I have something for you. It's out back."

"Jakob . . . "

He shook his head at her ever stubborn, independent attitude. "Just come take a look, Shiloh." They walked through the lobby and down the hallway to the back door which Jakob held open for her. Shiloh shivered as his hand touched the small of her back when she passed through the doorway. She gasped when saw the overflowing pots.

"Oh, Jakob! These are gorgeous!"

"Do you like them?"

"Of course I like them! They are beautiful. But why did you make them?"

"I thought these two would look nice in your lobby, and I did this one for your office."

"Will you let me pay you for them?"

Jakob sighed. "Do you often let people pay for a gift you've given them, Shiloh?" He wheeled the pot for her office towards the door. "Why is it that you find it so difficult to believe that I might just want to do something nice for you?"

Shiloh held the door open but did not answer.

When Shiloh got home that afternoon, she was greeted by Jakob and Gavin. "Hi! What a lovely surprise."

"I was hoping I could crash here with Jakob for a few days. Is that okay with you?"

"Of course it's okay, Gavin. Don't be silly."

The three of them tackled the critter chores with Gavin and Shiloh chatting a mile a minute. Once all the chores were done, they headed into town for a bite to eat at The Tulip Diner. Shiloh loved being around Jakob and his family.

Falling

Jakob found her in the tack room of the barn. She had been checking on Aloysius, who wasn't doing well, after completing the outside chores. Shiloh was leaning heavily on the counter. "Hey, you okay?" he asked her from the doorway.

"Jakob, I don't feel well. I am really dizzy."

"Let me help. Let's get you inside."

"If it's a virus, I can give it to the pig and the ferrets."

"Then let's get you to my place, and I will call Jack so he can come by and take a look at you." He put his arm around her shoulders, intending to help her walk to the apartment. Shiloh lost her balance. "Okay, Shiloh. I've got you. Let me pick you up." Jakob knew she must be feeling poorly as she didn't protest. He easily scooped her up and carried her up the stairs then into his bedroom, laying her on the bed. "What can I get you?" He covered her with the quilt folded at the end of the bed.

"Nothing, thank you." She closed her eyes.

Jakob picked up his phone and dialed his brother. "Hey, are you home?"

"Yes. What's up?" Jack asked.

"Shiloh is sick. Can you come by? I am worried about her. She couldn't even make it from the barn to my place without me carrying her."

"Sure, I am on my way." Jakob put on a kettle and made tea while he waited for Jack.

"Hey, Shiloh," Jack said as he went to the side of the bed. "Not feeling too good?"

"Not good at all, Jack. Thanks for coming here. I'm not sure I could have made it to your office." Jack smiled. He completed his exam, determining that Shiloh had a severe case of the flu, likely spread from one of their mutual patients who had been in her office a few days before.

"You need rest, Shiloh. Lots of rest, fluids, healthy foods. I am going to give you Tamiflu, which should help lessen the symptoms a bit. You can use lozenges for sore throat and any kind of over-the-counter painkiller like Tylenol to help with the achy muscles. The most important thing is to stay hydrated." Shiloh nodded as she swallowed the flu medication. "Get some rest."

"Thank you, Jack."

Jack joined Jakob in the kitchen, leaving Shiloh to rest. "It's the flu. She should be fine, but she needs rest. Good luck with that," he said, smiling. Jakob laughed. Jack handed him two pills. "You need to take these so hopefully you don't get the same thing. Try to keep her hydrated as well. Her fever is pretty high, so she is definitely going to need plenty of fluids. If you think she is heading towards dehydration, call me so I can stop by and start an IV."

"Thanks, Jack. I will keep you posted."

Jack left and Jakob put together a tray with a pot of tea, cream, sugar, and a pitcher of water with a glass and went to the bedroom to check on Shiloh. "Can I make you a cup of tea?"

"That would be nice, thank you." Jakob poured her a cup.

"What would you like in it?"

"Milk and sugar, please." Shiloh repositioned herself so she was leaning against the pillows. "You don't have to wait on me, Jakob."

"You need your rest, and you can't be around Presley and the little guys, so you are stuck here with me. I have every intention of waiting on you and making sure that you get the rest that you need." Shiloh was too tired to fight with him. She sipped her tea.

Jakob took her cup when she was finished. "You need to get some rest. I will be right here, so if you need anything just holler." He poured her a glass of water, placing it on the nightstand. Shiloh snuggled into the bed, ready for some sleep.

"Thank you for taking care of me, Jakob." He smiled as he took the tray back to the kitchen. He picked up his phone and dialed his nephew, Braxton. Shiloh had hired him a couple of weeks before to help at the clinic. Brax was enrolled at the college in Barber, studying to become a vet tech.

"Hey, Uncle Jakob."

"Hey, Brax, how are things?"

"They are good. How about with you?"

"Good. I need your help though."
"Okay, what's up?"

"Shiloh is pretty sick with a severe case of the flu. I need you to clear her calendar for the next few days. I am going to call Drew to see if Dr. Ingram can take emergency calls for her, but everything else will need to get pushed back for at least three days, maybe longer, depending on how it goes. Are there any patients that are recovering at the clinic?"

"Yes, one dog that was neutered on Friday. The owners were traveling, so they opted to have Allegro stay with us for the weekend. They are picking the dog up Monday."

"Okay. I will see if Dr. Ingram can swing by there to officially discharge him. Are you good to go to get everything rescheduled? Oh, and can you water the plants in the lobby and in her office?"

"Sure, Uncle Jakob. I will take care of it."

"Thank you, Brax."

"Tell Shiloh I hope she feels better."

"I will."

Jakob dialed Drew. "Hello?"

"Hey. What's happening over there?"

"Not a lot, Jakob. What's happening with you?"

"Not much. Shiloh is under the weather, a bad case of the flu. That's why I am calling. I was hoping that maybe Isaac could take her emergencies for the next three or four days? Brax is pushing everything up to next week, but someone needs to be on call, and there is one patient that needs to be discharged by a vet before he can go home tomorrow."

"I hate to hear she is feeling bad. I will ask Isaac right now, I am sure he would be happy to cover. Can Brax meet him at the clinic for the discharge?"

"I'm sure he can. Just have Isaac reach out to him directly. Brax knows that I was going to get him to cover."

"Do you need anything? I can drop off something on my way out tonight."

"I think we are good. She is sleeping at the moment. I will try to get her to eat something soon. Jack has already been by, so I think we have it covered, but thank you."

Jakob left the apartment and went to check on the pig and the dogs. It was a nice day, so he opted to put them out in their respective areas. He checked food and water bowls, scooped boxes, and gave everyone a few minutes of attention. The inside gang seemed to be doing well.

On his way back to the apartment, he stopped by the barn to see Aloysius. "Hey, bud. How are you feeling?" he asked softly, scratching the horse behind the ears. "Your mom isn't feeling too great, so I am going to be taking care of you for the next few days, okay?" Aloysius nuzzled Jakob's arm. "That means you are going to need to be a good boy for me. You need to eat your dinner and let me give you your medication. You can't do anything that might stress your mom out. Deal?" The horse gave him a snort. Jakob chuckled. "I'll be back tonight, big guy. I gotta go check on your mom."

As Jakob left the barn, his sister-in-law's car pulled up in the driveway. "Hey, Ange! What are you doing here?"

"Hey yourself!" she said. "Drew called and said that Shiloh was under the weather, so I thought I would make some soups. She can't get better on your specialties of biscuits and gravy and scrambled egg sandwiches." She kissed his cheek. "You are many wonderful things, Jakob, but chef does not happen to be one of them." Jakob smiled as they climbed the stairs to the apartment. Drew and Jakob were three years apart. He, Angelica, and Drew went through school together and had known each other for a very long time.

They went to the kitchen and Ange unloaded the bag of goodies she had brought, putting the containers into the fridge. "I brought three kinds of soup and a couple of choices for bread. I also picked up juice and some stuff for your medicine cabinet. I am guessing you don't have cough drops or cough syrup on hand?"

Jakob smiled. "You take good care of me," he said, giving her a quick hug. The two chatted for a few minutes before Angelica left for home. Jakob went to check on Shiloh.

She stirred as he sat on the edge of the bed. "Hi there. How are you feeling?"

"Like I got hit by a truck."

Jakob smiled. "I know. I'm sorry. Let's get some fluids in you. Are you hungry? Ange brought you some soup."

"Not hungry."

"I hear you, but it's not really optional. Do you want water, tea, or juice?"

Shiloh sighed. "Water, I guess." Jakob poured her a glass from the pitcher on the nightstand.

"Down the hatch." Shiloh sat up and took the glass. "I'm going to heat up a small cup of soup for you. Do you want chicken noodle, lentil, or vegetable beef?"

"Lentil, please." He went to the kitchen and put some soup in a mug, heating it in the microwave. When he went back into the bedroom, the bed was empty. He waited for a couple of minutes and then went to the bathroom door, knocking softly.

"You okay in there?" he asked. The bathroom door opened to a miserable-looking Shiloh. She was sweating, there were dark circles under her eyes, and she looked exhausted. "Oh, Shiloh, come here." He put his arms around her shoulders, feeling her lean heavily against him. He scooped her into his arms and carried her back to the bed. He laid her back against the pillows and sat next to her. He brushed the hair from her damp forehead. "Try to eat for me?"

She nodded and he handed her the cup of soup. "This is very good," she said after only a few bites.

"Yeah, Ange is quite the cook. All of my sisters-in-law are actually." He took her cup and handed her the water. "Are you achy? I have some painkillers here," he said, reaching for the bottle.

"Okay." He handed her two tablets and she took the pills with the last of her water.

"Back to bed." Shiloh scooted down, finding a comfortable position as Jakob covered her with the quilt.

"Thank you, Jakob," she said, her voice almost a whisper. He checked on her several times over the course of the afternoon, letting her get some much-needed rest.

It was early evening when Jakob went out to start the evening rounds. He decided to take care of the inside critters first. He fed the pig, the dogs, and the cat then moved on to the little ones, performing the necessary chores and administering the medications from Shiloh's meticulous notes. Everyone inside was settled for the evening. Next, he went to corral the birds, getting them into the coop and locked down for the night. He spent some time playing with the dogs, throwing the ball and frisbee for them and then getting them indoors and settled. He was thankful that all the kitties were in attendance. He didn't want a repeat of a few nights ago where they had to search to find one of them. He fed the cats, scooped the litter boxes, freshened their water, and gave each of them a short session with a brush.

When he moved on to the livestock, he found that Aloysius had gone down. After several tries to get him back on his feet, Jakob gave him a break while he got the other animals into their stalls and fed. He went back to the horse and tried again. Apparently, his illness had progressed to the end stage. He picked up the phone and dialed Shiloh's office number, knowing it would connect him to Dr. Ingram. Jakob explained the situation to Isaac, who was immediately en route to Shiloh's farm. Jakob then called Drew and explained the situation, asking for help dealing with the horse's remains once he had been put down. Drew assured him he would take care of it; he and his team would be over as soon as possible.

Dr. Ingram arrived and confirmed Jakob's worst fears: the horse needed to be put down. Shortly after, Drew and his team arrived ready to take care of things. Jakob slowly trudged up the stairs to wake Shiloh and give her the news. It was a conversation he dreaded. It was going to be hard enough for her to lose her beloved horse, but having it happen while she was this sick was just unfair.

"Shiloh," he said softly. She opened her eyes.

"Hi."

"How are you feeling?"

"About the same, I think." She stretched, her body aching even with the pain relievers.

"Shiloh, I need to tell you something." She sat up in the bed, sensing it was bad news. "It's Aloysius. He's down. I think it's time for you to say your goodbyes." Shiloh's eyes filled with tears. While she wasn't surprised given the state of the horse's health, it didn't make letting him go any easier. Jakob reached for his jacket hanging on the back of the door and helped her put it on. He helped her to her feet, holding her hand. Her legs were still weak and wobbly; without giving her an option, Jakob picked her up and carried her down the stairs and into the barn. He set her down in the stall with the horse, helping her sit and gently putting the horse's head in her lap. "I'll give you a few minutes with him."

"Jakob, I don't think I can do this. You know, give him the shot."

"Oh, Shiloh," he said, squatting down next to her. His hand gently rubbed her back. "No one would expect you to be able to do that. Dr. Ingram is here and will do whatever is necessary when you're ready." Shiloh nodded, tears streaming down her cheeks. He stood to leave as she reached for his hand.

"Thank you, Jakob." He squeezed her hand right before he left the stall. Shiloh spent about twenty minutes with Aloysius, scratching him in all his favorite spots and whispering in his ear about how much she loved him and what a good boy he had been for her. When she couldn't take it anymore, she called for Jakob.

"Are you ready?" he asked her, his voice soft and kind. She nodded. Jakob motioned for Dr. Ingram. He came into the stall, quietly giving his condolences to Shiloh as he got into position and prepared the injection. "Do you want me to stay?" Jakob asked.

"Yes," she whispered. Jakob sat down next to her, his arm around her shoulders, his hand stroking the horse's nose. Drew watched silently from outside the stall, fascinated in the transformation of his brother since leaving Delilah. He hadn't seen the caring and kind side of Jakob in years, and it was evident that he had strong feelings for Shiloh. Dr. Ingram administered the injection and everyone collectively held their breath until they had confirmation that the horse had passed. Jakob stood and stepped out of the stall, giving Shiloh a last few minutes alone with her horse.

"Keep this up and you are going to challenge me for my title," Drew joked with him. Drew was considered the "nicest Cooke," a title which he hated but had carried ever since childhood.

Jakob laughed. "Don't worry, brother, your crown is safe."

After a few minutes, Jakob stepped into the stall. He picked her up without a word and carried her upstairs. Shiloh held onto his shoulders tightly as he laid her on the bed. "Please don't go," she whispered.

"I'm not going anywhere. Let's get you comfortable first." He helped her take the jacket off and pulled the covers around her as she laid back against the pillows. Jakob poured her another glass of water and handed her two more pain relievers. She took them without protest and drank all the water. "Do you want me to make you something to eat?"

"No, thank you. I just want to sleep."

"Okay, then try to get comfortable." Shiloh tried but her muscles hurt too much. Jakob kicked off his shoes and pulled off his sweatshirt. He laid down next to her. "Come here, Shiloh." She rolled towards him, feeling his arms go around her. She tried to hold back the flood of tears but could not. She was too heartbroken over the loss of Aloysius and she felt too awful to put on her usual brave face. She felt his arms tighten around her, drawing her closer. "It's okay, my Fia," he whispered as he kissed the top of her head.

"What name is that?" she asked sleepily.

"Fia? When I was stationed at Mildenhall in the UK, I spent a lot of my free time in Ireland. In Ireland, the name Fia means a flickering flame." he explained. "It fits you in several ways." Jakob rubbed her back and held her close until she drifted off to sleep. He heard a soft knock at the door and then heard it open. Jack came into the bedroom.

"Drew called. How is she?"

"She's heartbroken and feels awful. The timing just sucks, Jack."

"I know. I'm sorry she's going through this. It looks like the two of you are getting pretty close." Jack shot him the famous look with an eyebrow raised and an evil grin as if to say "prove me wrong."

Jakob smiled. "Don't be fooled. This is only because she isn't feeling well. I am pretty sure once she's over the flu, her same stubborn ways will be back."

"Maybe they will, but then again, maybe they won't. Call me if you need anything." Jack left, locking up and heading home for the night.

Jakob woke the next morning before Shiloh. He quietly slipped out of bed and went to the kitchen to make tea and something for her to eat. He checked on her one more time before starting his chores, thinking to himself how beautiful she looked sleeping in his bed. He did his chores outside and inside, giving each of the animals individual attention as he cared for them. He checked the mail, watered Shiloh's plants, washed the few dishes she had in her sink, found a pair of clean pajamas for her, and went back to the apartment. When he arrived, she was up and in the shower. He knocked and poked his head into the steamy bathroom. "I brought you some clean pajamas. I'll just leave them here on the counter."

"Thank you, Jakob," she said from behind the curtain.

Jakob went to the kitchen, got breakfast out of the fridge, and poured two cups of tea. Shiloh joined him shortly after, looking a little better than the previous day but still obviously not feeling well. "How are you feeling this morning?"

"Like I just ran a marathon. Who knew taking a shower could be so strenuous? How are the animals?"

"Everyone looks good. Chores for the morning are done and no one seemed to have any complaints."

"Presley?"

"The pig is just fine, Shiloh. He has had his breakfast and is playing outside until the sun gets to his spot and then I will put him in." Shiloh sipped her tea and took a bite of fruit. She wasn't at all hungry but knew she needed to try to eat something.

"Jakob, I need to make arrangements . . . " Her voice broke.

He went to her, embracing her tightly. "Shiloh, Drew and his team took care of that last night. They picked a spot way back in the pastures, close to the trees. I hope that's okay." She nodded, her arms tightening around his waist.

"Thank you."

"It wasn't any trouble. You should finish your breakfast. I thought maybe you would want to rest out here on the couch for a bit? You could watch a movie while I do a quick change of the bed."

"I can change the sheets, Jakob."

"You are under strict orders from my brother, the doctor, to rest. He stopped by yesterday to check on you, by the way. I'm not going to go against his orders. He's cranky when he doesn't get his way."

Shiloh smiled. She had a hard time imagining Jack being cranky. They finished breakfast and Shiloh settled in on the couch with remote in hand. Jakob stripped the bed, remade it, and put a load of laundry in the washer. "I need to run out for a couple of hours to take some photos at a client's place. Are you going to be okay here by yourself?"

"I have the flu. I am not an invalid. I will be fine. You go do what you need to and I will lie around."

He smiled. "The bed is ready if you want to take a nap."

"Thank you, Jakob. I really appreciate you taking such good care of me."

"I like taking care of you, Shiloh," he said, closing the door behind him. Shiloh's heart skipped a beat. She could feel herself losing control, and those feelings terrified her. She didn't want to fall in love with anyone. She wasn't prepared to let anyone hurt her again.

Jakob met with his client and took the photos he needed to work on the design. His phone rang. It was Chance. "Hey."

"Hey. How's Shiloh?"

"She's okay, I think. Still feeling crappy and dealing with the horse thing."

"I hope she starts feeling better soon. Waverly has been in the kitchen. I have some things to drop off. You know she thinks everyone needs to kill their germs with an overdose of baked goods." Jakob chuckled.

"I'm actually out and about. I can stop by and pick them up if that's easier."

"Sure, that works."

"Okay, I'll be by in twenty minutes or so."

As he drove through town, he stopped off at The Perfect Petals to buy Shiloh some flowers. "Hey, Lark."

"Jakob, hi! How are you? How is Shiloh?" *Oh the joys of small-town living,* he thought to himself.

"She's getting better. Thanks for asking. I want to pick up some flowers to cheer her up."

"Sure. Everything in the case is available, or I can put something together for you if none of those strike your fancy." Jakob looked at the choices, finding a beautiful large bouquet full of lavender roses, alstroemeria, purple carnations, asters, chrysanthemums, snapdragons, bells of Ireland, huckleberry, and lemon leaf.

"I'll take this one," he said as he pulled it from the refrigerated case.

"I saw Delilah yesterday." She was trying to get a rise out of him. Jakob's ex-wife was one of her close friends.

"That's nice."

"She's doing really well, you know."

"Happy to hear it." He paid for the flowers and quickly exited the store. The last thing he wanted to hear or think about was Delilah. Jakob stopped by Chance's farm office, picked up the box of goodies, and drove back to the apartment to check on Shiloh.

Jakob set the flowers on the counter along with the box. Shiloh wasn't in the living room. He poked his head into the bedroom and found her fast asleep in the bed. Back in the kitchen he unloaded brownies, cookies, a peach cobbler, strawberries for shortcake along with an angel food cake, and a cherry pie from the box. How much did Waverly think they could eat? Jakob put the cobbler, strawberries, and pie into the fridge and pulled out the chicken noodle soup. He put it in a pot on the stove to let it heat and poured two glasses of juice. He was worried that she hadn't eaten much, and he wasn't sure she was taking in enough fluids.

He set the flowers on the nightstand and sat next to her on the bed, softly feeling her forehead with the back of his hand. Shiloh's eyes slowly opened. "Hey, you. How are you feeling?"

"Better, I think. Are those for me?" she asked with a smile. "They're beautiful."

"Of course they are for you, silly girl. I was hoping they might cheer you up. But for now, I need you to get up and come eat some lunch." Shiloh groaned. "It's not optional. Let's move."

Jakob helped her up and held her hand as he guided her to the barstool at the kitchen island. He handed her a glass of juice and went to the stove to get the bowls of soup. Shiloh sipped her juice, watching him maneuver around the kitchen. She was starting to have feelings for him despite her desperate internal battle to prevent them. "Eat up, please," he said as he placed the bowls on the island. Shiloh ate the first bite then it hit her just how hungry she was. Jakob watched, amused, as she devoured the bowl of soup and requested a second helping. She topped off her lunch with a brownie.

"Okay, I am stuffed and exhausted. It's so frustrating. I didn't do anything, and yet I feel like I just climbed a mountain."
"Don't worry. You will get your strength back soon enough. How about we watch a movie?"

"Okay. What should we watch?"

Jakob helped her to the couch and handed her the remote.

"You choose. I'll be right back after I put the soup away." He tidied the kitchen and refilled Shiloh's juice glass. Shiloh flipped through the channels and found a George Clooney movie. "Oh, I see how it is," Jakob joked as he set her glass on the coffee table.

"Scoot over." He laid down next to her, his arms around her shoulders. "Is this okay?"

Shiloh smiled and nodded as she snuggled against him. Jakob pulled the afghan from the back of the sofa and draped it over them. It didn't take long for her to fall asleep. Jakob turned off the television and picked up a book he was reading. He was content just to be close to her. She slept for several hours and only stirred for a moment as Jakob slipped out of the apartment to complete the evening chores.

He returned, deciding to let her continue to sleep while he ate a banana and then a handful of cookies. He scooped Shiloh into his arms and carried her into the bedroom.

"Jakob?" she whispered groggily.

"Right here, Shiloh." He laid her on the bed then snuggled next to her, holding her close. He felt her arms go around him as she nestled into his embrace.

"I like it here with you."

"I like it here with you too, Fia," he said as he kissed her hair, breathing in its scent.

Shiloh quickly fell back into a fever-induced sleep. Jakob tried, but could not turn off the thoughts running through his head: *I think I am in love with her. Is it too soon to feel this way? I could get used to this.* At last, sleep found him.

Shiloh woke the early the next morning, feeling better than she had in days and still wrapped firmly in Jakob's embrace. She laid still, smelling the faint remnants of his cologne, feeling the slow and steady rhythm of his breathing, and hearing his heartbeat as her head rested against his chest. She felt more content than she had in years, yet the fear gnawing at the pit of her stomach could not be ignored.

As she watched him, his eyes opened and a smile spread across his face. "Good morning." His hand caressed her cheek, his fingers tucking her hair behind her ear. He leaned in, his lips pressing softly against hers. Shiloh felt her stomach flutter and her heart rate start to climb. Her head told her to pull back, to run from him. Her heart, her body responded in a different way all together. Jakob pulled her closer as Shiloh returned the kiss. Finally the fear and anxiety won over the pleasure. "Jakob . . . " She pulled away from him. "I can't. I can't fall in love with you." Her voice was just a whisper.

"Would it be that bad?"

"Jakob, I am broken, beyond repair. You don't deserve someone with this much baggage."

"Everyone has baggage, Shiloh. Tell me why you think you are broken." Her eyes welled up with tears. Jakob held her closer.

"I can't. I have never told anyone."

"All the more reason. Your secrets are safe with me, sweetheart. Please, tell me." Shiloh was silent, her mind racing, wanting to share with him but so afraid of what he would think.

"I was with someone," she whispered timidly. "He was . . . it was not a good thing. He said things, awful things. He hit me. A lot." Jakob tightened his hold around her, kissing the top of her head. "He forced me . . . " she choked out the words, followed by a sob.

"Okay, it's okay, sweetheart," he held her tightly. He felt the burn of rage in his belly. The thought of someone hurting her was almost more that he could bear. "You're safe now, safe with me."

"That's just it. I'm not. I haven't been with him in years. But, every now and then he sends me something. Something to let me know he is watching, that he knows where I am."

Jakob tried to take in what she was saying. "How long has it been since you heard from him?"

"I don't know, maybe six weeks."

"I'm going to talk to Karl about options."

"Thank you, but I'm not sure there are any options, Jakob," she said glumly.

"So, that's it? That's the baggage?"

"That's the source of the baggage. I can't be close to anyone. I don't trust people. You deserve someone who can let you in, someone with more experience than me. Someone who doesn't have a crazy ex that won't go away."

"You haven't been with anyone since him?" She shook her head no.

"Or before him." Jakob felt a twinge in his heart. The thought of the only relationship she had experienced being one filled with anger and abuse made him incredibly sad. He held her for a few minutes, both of them silent, lost in their own thoughts.

"I'm feeling better. I should go, let you get your life back." She pulled away from his embrace and got out of bed. She was still a bit weak and unsteady.

"Shiloh . . . " he followed her into the living room. "You are not over the flu and you know it." He stepped towards her, his arms going around her waist. "Please, sweetheart, I know you're scared. You don't need to be. We can go slow." His voice was so soft. She felt his lips softly brush hers. He felt her pull away again. She turned and walked towards the door. "Shiloh, please don't walk away."

He watched the front door close behind her. It took everything he had not to go after her, but he knew she needed some time. He took a lengthy shower, dressed, and went to start on the morning chores. He took care of the birds, the outside cats and dogs, and then walked to her house to see if she needed help with the inside animals. He knocked on the door and waited, but there was no answer. He opened the door and called her name. Nothing. He had assumed she was going to the house; now he was concerned about where she was. He knew she still wasn't feeling well. He quickly cared for the littlest animals and got the dogs, the pig, and the cat situated. He walked to the barn, wondering to himself where she could have gone. He found her in Aloysius's stall, knees drawn up to her chest, tears streaming down her cheeks.

Jakob sighed. "Don't go anywhere," he said as he walked past her, fed the livestock, and put them outdoors for the day.

Jakob sat down next to her, putting his arm around her shoulders. She looked miserable. "Jakob . . . "

"Hush. We aren't going to talk about this now. You are going to let me take you back upstairs and care for you until you are actually over this flu. Then we can chat. Deal?" Shiloh nodded. Jakob scooped her up and carried her upstairs, laying her on the bed.

"Please don't be angry with me."

"I'm not angry with you, Shiloh. You need to get some rest, sweetheart."

"Please stay." Jakob smiled as he laid down next to her, feeling her curl up into his embrace. Maybe there was hope for them after all. Shiloh slept soundly for several hours, waking in the early afternoon, still in his arms.

"How are you feeling?"

"Better, I think." Jakob kissed her gently, feeling her respond. He kissed her again with more passion.

"Just tell me we can go slow, sweetheart," he said gently. He felt her tense, her body pull away from his.

"I can't, Jakob. I'm sorry. I want to, but I can't." She got out of bed and closed the door behind her as she went into the bathroom. She sighed heavily as she leaned against the counter after turning the shower on. She wanted him so desperately, more than she had ever wanted a man before, but fear won out. Its power outweighed the desire, and she knew she needed to stay away from him for a while. She showered, dressed, and went into the living room.

"Do you want some dinner?"

"No, thank you. Jakob. I am feeling better, so I think it would be best if I went home. I appreciate you taking care of me and the sanctuary, but I think it would be best if you and I went back to the way things were before."

"I'm not sure we can do that, Shiloh." He stepped towards her, his hands on her cheeks as he tipped her chin, kissing her softly.

She stepped away from him. "I have to go." She turned and walked away. Jakob sighed as she closed the door behind her.

Shiloh spent the next two days going through the motions. She returned to work, seeing a full load of animal patients. She took care of the indoor critters and let Jakob continue to handle things outside. She didn't have the physical stamina or the emotional strength to give in to what she really wanted or to push him away completely. Jakob reached out several times via phone and text. She didn't answer as she didn't know what to say. She was miserable.

About 11:30 that evening, she couldn't take it anymore. She put on shoes and walked the short distance between her house and Jakob's apartment. She knocked softly on his door. Jakob answered, surprised to see her. "Did I wake you?"

"No, I was watching the news. Are you okay? Do I need to call Jack or something?" She shook her head no as her eyes welled up with tears. She prided herself on always being in control, but Jakob had the power to make her feel weak and vulnerable.

"Come here," he said, holding out his arms. She went to him, her arms going around him tightly.

"I feel stuck."

He closed the door behind her as he kissed her forehead. "I'm not sure what that means, sweetheart."

"I am too afraid to go forward and I can't figure out how to go back. I'm stuck and unhappy and I don't know how to fix it." Tears rolled down her cheeks.

"We can go slow, Shiloh. I promise you that I can be a very patient man." He brushed away her tears.

"Okay," she whispered. He softly kissed her lips.

"There are a couple other promises I'd like to make you. I'm not sure if you know, but the Cookes never break their promises." Shiloh smiled.

"I promise you that there is nothing, not one thing, that you could do or say that would ever result in me raising a hand to you. I mean it, Shiloh, never. And, I promise you that one day, whenever that is, when you let me make love to you, I will do everything in my power to please you. And, for the time being, I will do everything in my power to make you fall in love with me."

"I don't know what to say."

"You don't need to say anything." He kissed her again. "Are you staying here with me tonight?"

"If that's okay with you. I haven't been able to sleep without you." He smiled as he led her into the bedroom.

The next morning they woke, did the morning chores together, had a bite to eat, and went their separate ways for the day. Midmorning, Jakob pulled up in the alley behind the building Jack and Shiloh shared and found the two of them outside chatting over a cup of tea. Jakob got out of the truck with an enormous bouquet of flowers. Jack grinned as Shiloh blushed.

"Hey," Jakob said as he tenderly kissed her lips.

"Hi," she said, a huge smile on her face, her heart pounding. "They're beautiful, Jakob. Thank you. Let me get them in some water." She turned and went into the clinic to find a vase.

Jack smiled. "I'm happy for you, for both of you," he said. Jakob was practically beaming.

"I haven't been this happy in as long as I can remember, Jack."

"I can see that."

"Do you guys come out here often?"

"Couple of times a week, I guess. Why?"

"No reason. Hey, I gotta go. I have a new client." He opened the door to Shiloh's office and found her arranging the mass of flowers. "Sweetheart, I have to go to meet a new client. I will see you tonight and I'll take care of dinner," he said as he held her. He kissed her and turned for the door.

"Thank you for the flowers, Jakob." He winked at her and the door closed behind him. Shiloh had a difficult time thinking of much else besides Jakob for the rest of the afternoon. She was still terribly afraid, but she couldn't help but enjoy the attention and the new feelings she was having for him. They met at home that evening and did chores together then ate Chinese and spent the rest of the evening curled up on her sofa watching television until they went to bed.

Midafternoon, both Jack and Shiloh were startled by a loud banging at the back of the building. They both went to their back doors to see what was going on to find Jakob there, installing an awning between their two doors. "Um, Jakob, what are you doing?" Jack asked.

"I figured if you guys come out here a couple of times a week to have tea, I should make it a bit nicer for you." Jack smiled, shook his head, and went back inside to see his next patient.

"You didn't have to do this, Jakob." Shiloh was still shocked at all that he was willing to do for her.

Jakob put down the drill and put his arm around her waist. "I didn't do this because I had to, Shiloh. I did it because I like doing things for you. You are just going to have to get used to it." He kissed her softy and then resumed his work. "You go back inside and do what you were doing. I'll call you when I am done." Shiloh went back to her office and pretended to work, but she couldn't concentrate. There were all sorts of noises happening outside her door. It took all of her willpower to keep from peeking.

Finally, after what felt like forever but was really just over an hour, Jakob poked his head through the doorway. "Are you ready to come take a look?"

"Yes!" She practically jumped up from her desk. Jakob held the door for her. What she saw when she went out to the alley took her breath away. Jakob had installed a black-and-white striped awning between the two rear doors. Underneath the awning, sat a black metal table with four chairs. The cushions were white with a black floral print. There were large black pots bursting with plants and flowers in different shades of red. There were hanging pots in the corners of the awnings dripping with red blooms and there was a stunning arrangement as the centerpiece for the table. Underfoot lay a white, red, and black floral rug. "Jakob!"

"Do you like it?"

She threw her arms around his neck and kissed him. "It's beautiful! Thank you so much! We have to get Jack." Jakob stuck his head in the door to Jack's office and called his name. After a minute or two, he joined them in the alley.

"Wow! Jakob, this looks fantastic. I like reaping the benefits of you trying to sweep Shiloh off her feet. Keep up the good work!" Jack grinned his famous evil grin as Jakob and Shiloh laughed.

Braxton stuck his head out the door. "Shiloh, your appointment is here. Hey, Uncle Jakob. Hey, Uncle Jack."

Shiloh gave Jakob a quick kiss. "Thank you. I'll see you at home. My turn to do dinner."

Shiloh floated through the afternoon feeling insanely happy. After her last appointment wrapped up, she sent Braxton home early and closed up shop. She stopped by Wagonner's to pick up a few groceries so she could make dinner for Jakob and do the bulk of the chores before he got home.

Jakob came through the door, greeting the pig as he came in. He found Shiloh in the kitchen finishing up dinner. He put his arms around her as he stood behind her, kissing her neck. "That smells amazing, sweetheart." He nuzzled her neck again, "I missed you."

She turned to face him, her arms going around his shoulders. "I missed you too." He kissed her softly at first and then with more passion, taking her breath away. "Jakob . . . "

"Do I have time to grab a shower before dinner?"

Shiloh nodded. He went to his apartment, showered, and changed. When he went back to Shiloh's, she had set the table and lit some candles. "Can you open the wine?" she called to him from the kitchen. He popped the cork and poured them each a glass as Shiloh came through the door with plates filled with lasagna, garlic bread, and salad. They ate, chatted, and laughed through the meal. Shiloh tackled the kitchen while Jakob finished the chores outside. They settled in on the couch and flipped through the channels. Shiloh dozed, content, as Jakob watched the news.

Jakob and Shiloh had a great time with Jack and Penni at the Fall Fest, but they were both glad to be home and off the treacherous roads. They took care of chores, getting the animals settled in for the storm then curled up together on the sofa. It didn't take long for Shiloh to doze off. Jakob flipped through the channels trying to find something that caught his interest. It was just before midnight when his cell phone rang. It was Karl . . .

THE PRECARIOUS ROAD

It was no one's fault really, this series of events that created a disaster and left three lives in the balance. Emanating from those three lives, the effects rippled outwards exponentially. Some might call it fate, others being in the wrong place at the wrong time. Karl Arnold came upon the accident site as the first on scene. Upon his arrival, he was unaware of his close ties to the victims, but it didn't take long for him to realize who they were. His heart sank. He called for additional ambulances and tried to assess the severity of the injuries, not wanting to have to move any of the occupants of the car before the paramedics arrived. It was quiet, just the rain falling and instantly freezing on everything it touched without making any sound. It felt like an eternity that he was there alone.

At last, he could hear the sirens in the distance. While the ambulances crawled to the scene of the accident on the frozen roadways, Karl moved through the rubble to the engine of the train and discovered that the engineer was deceased. He radioed that a coroner was needed. Karl slipped, going down on one knee as he tried to make it back to the vehicle. Once there, he checked vitals again. Everyone in the car was still alive, but he wasn't sure for how long, They were in pretty bad shape. Sheriff Paul Mason pulled up with three ambulances following.

"Arnold, what do we have?"

"Hey, boss. It appears that the train was going fast, too fast for the conditions. Ice had built up on the crossing. The vehicle was sitting at the crossing, waiting for the train to pass when it derailed, plowing into the car. It looks like eight or nine train cars derailed. Engineer is dead. The three victims in the car aren't in great shape. Two of them are Cooke kids. The other is the Creswell kid."

One of the difficult things about living in a small community is that when tragedy strikes, the victims are people you know. The paramedics were extricating the injured, loading them into the waiting ambulances, and preparing for the treacherous trip to the nearest hospital in Barber.

"You take the Cookes, and I will drive to Barber to inform the Creswells," Paul suggested. Karl nodded. "Be careful, Karl, these conditions are terrible."

"Yeah, you too. I'll check in later." The two men got into their respective vehicles, leaving another deputy to deal with the scene and the incoming NTSB team who would need to investigate the accident. Before he pulled away from the scene, he picked up his cell phone and dialed his closest friend.

"I bet your night sucks. This weather is nuts," Jakob answered.

"Jakob . . . " The hair on the back of Jakob's neck stood up. He instantly knew something was very wrong. He gently slipped away from Shiloh, who was sleeping on the sofa, and went to the kitchen.

"What's happened?"

Karl paused, dreading having to share the news with his friend.

"Karl?"

"There's been an accident. I'd like to come pick you up so we can tell Chance and Drew together." Jakob felt nauseous, so much so he bent over the kitchen sink. "Jakob?"

"Kylie or Cassie?" Jakob asked.

"I'm pretty sure it's Kylie. Rowan Cresswell was in the car with her and Brax."

"How bad?"

"Pretty bad. I don't have the details. Paramedics left while I was briefing Paul."

"How long until you get here?"

"Twenty minutes maybe."

"Okay, I'll be ready." Jakob hung up the phone, shaken. He went to the living room to wake Shiloh. "Sweetheart, wake up," he said gently. Shiloh opened her eyes and sat up, not sure what the look on Jakob's face meant.

"Jakob, are you all right?'

"There's been an accident. My niece, her boyfriend, and my nephew were in the car. Karl is on his way over to pick me up so we can go and tell Drew and Chance."

"Oh God, that's awful. What can I do?"

"Just stay put, Shiloh. I don't know how long I will be." Shiloh nodded, taking his hands in hers.

"I'm so sorry, Jakob. I hope everyone is going to be okay. Did Karl say how badly they were injured?"

"He said it was bad but didn't have any details." Jakob stood and paced, worried, ready for Karl to arrive so they could get to his brothers and give them the news. Shiloh went to the kitchen to make some coffee.

At last, Karl arrived, trying to get to the door without falling on the icy path and steps. Jakob met him at the door and the two men went to the kitchen to say goodbye to Shiloh. She had two travel cups of coffee ready to go. "Please be careful, Jakob. And keep me posted, no matter what time." He kissed her gently, picked up the two cups of coffee, handing one to Karl, and headed for the door. She followed them, watching Karl slowly pull away.

"Let's stop and pick up Jack on the way. Everyone will want him at the hospital so he can decode the medical stuff."

They pulled into Jack's farm. "Sit tight. I will grab him and we can go."

Jakob carefully walked across the icy ground to the door and explained the situation to Jack, who grabbed a jacket and followed his brother back to the car.

A high level of tension filled the car on the drive to Chance and Waverly's. Karl was focused on the road, the conditions continuing to deteriorate. Jakob was worried about his family, not looking forward to showing up on his brother's doorstep to give him terrible news. Jack made a call to the hospital in Barber but was unable to get any information as the three victims were still in the emergency room being assessed.

"You okay?" Karl asked Jakob.

"Not really. What happened? Were there others who were injured?"

"It's a crazy thing, Jakob. They were sitting at the train crossing at Pearl Place. The train came through going too fast for conditions, flew off the tracks, and hit them."

"The engineer?"

"Dead. Guessing some sort of medical issue because there is no way that hitting a car should have killed him. Maybe he was dead before they got into town which is why there was no slowing? It was a fluke thing, Jakob."

"Who was driving?" Jack asked.

"Rowan. Kylie was in the front passenger seat and Brax in the back." Jakob swallowed hard, trying to keep himself pulled together. The drive that normally took about twenty minutes took them closer to forty-five. Karl pulled into the driveway of the Crescent Canyon Farm and parked but left the motor running with the defroster on high to keep the windshield clear of ice. The three men sat, silently dreading what was about to happen for a moment before Jakob opened the door and stepped onto the frozen ground, his foot crunching on the ice. The porch light flipped on. Chance was evidently waiting for Kylie to return. They carefully walked the concrete path to the front porch, navigating up the steps without incident. Chance opened the door before they had an opportunity to ring the bell.

"What's happened?" he demanded. Waverly came up behind him.

"Let them in, Chance. It's freezing out there." Chance stood aside as Karl, Jack, and Jakob went into the cozy living room.

"Where is she?" Chance asked, the panic in his voice discernable.

"They've taken her to Barber Regional," Karl said softly,

"What happened?" Waverly asked, her eyes glassy with tears. Jakob stepped towards her, putting his arms around her shoulders.

"It was a freak accident. They were waiting for the train to pass and it derailed because of the ice, hitting their car," Jakob explained.

"Is she . . . " Chance couldn't even say the word.

"We don't have an update, but she was still alive when the paramedics pulled her from the car," Karl answered.

"Mom, what's going on? What are you doing here, Uncle Jakob, Uncle Jack?" Cassie came into the room wearing her pajamas. Jakob cringed. She was way too young to have to deal with this.

"Go get dressed, Cassie. Your sister has been in an accident. We need to go." Chance's voice was hoarse with emotion. Waverly stood and followed Cassie out of the room. "It's my fault."

"Chance, it's no one's fault."

"I was at the Fall Fest. I should have insisted they ride with me."

"No one knew how bad it was out there, Chance. There was no reason for you to think their drive home would be anything but ordinary," Jakob said, putting his hand on his brother's shoulder. Chance went to the hall closet, pulling out his jacket and putting it on. He picked up his keys.

"I think you should let Karl drive you, Chance. It's terrible out there and you are in no condition to drive. Give me your keys, Jack, and I will pick up Ange and Drew and we will meet at the hospital," Jakob suggested as he held out his hand for the keys. Chance was too shaken to argue. Waverly and Cassie came into the room ready to go. Karl and Jakob helped the women to the car as Chance followed behind them. Jakob and Jack went to the garage, choosing the Kia Sportage that the girls shared to drive to Drew's. It was all-wheel drive. He thought it might do better in the hazardous conditions than Chance's old farm truck or Waverly's El Camino. The two got in the car, backed out of the garage, and set out on the short drive to Drew and Angelica's house.

"Can you call again?" Jakob, his hands white-knuckled on the wheel, asked as he drove. The conditions were horrible and not knowing how Kylie, Brax, and Rowan were doing was driving him crazy.

"Sure," Jack said, happy to have something to do. The report from the hospital was vague. All three were being assessed and there was no information available as the doctors were in with them, actively treating their injuries. When Jack pressed the nurse to tell them a condition for each, she came back with one word: critical. Jack sighed and thanked her for the information.

"Well?" Jackob asked, unsure if he really wanted to know the answer.

"No details. Docs are in with them now. Nurse says all three are critical." Jakob pulled into the drive off of River Road and parked.

"Let's go," he said as they got out of the car.

Angelica answered the door in pajamas, having fallen asleep on the couch. Jakob explained the situation as gently as he could, holding her tightly as she cried.

"Go change. We will pick up Drew and get to the hospital," Jakob said. She went to the bedroom to find something to wear, almost on autopilot.

"It's weird to think of them being apart," Jakob said to Jack, referring to the issues Ange and Drew were having. Jack sighed and nodded, thinking to himself that this would either bring them back together or further pull them apart. Ange returned and the three of them loaded up and started their journey to the inn.

It was a treacherous drive across their little town. They passed several cars off the road on their way, all of them empty. The rain had let up for the time being, but every surface was coated with several inches of ice. Jakob pulled under the portico by the front door and parked. Angelica was in tears in the backseat.

"You go. We'll wait here," Jack said, getting out of the front seat and climbing into the back to comfort his sister-in-law. Jakob went in and rang the bell. After a minute or two Neal came to the desk yawning.

"Jakob! What can I do for you?"

"I'm sorry to bother you so late. I need to talk to Drew. It's important."

"Of course. He's in the Wisteria Room, the upstairs room of the cottage. Right this way. Paxton is here too in the Daffodil Room. Oh, and Elizabeth is in one of the guest rooms in the house. Should I wake her?"

"Yes, please." Neal knocked on Paxton's door as Jakob went up the stairs to Drew's room. Paxton joined them upstairs.

"What's going on, Jakob?" Drew demanded. Jakob explained the situation and answered the questions Drew and Pax had the best that he could. Elizabeth joined them, giving each of them a hug.

"Everything is going to be okay," she said to Drew.

"Jack and Ange are downstairs in the car. Get dressed and we can head to the hospital. It's going to take us some time to get there." Jakob and Elizabeth went downstairs to the car. Jack and Ange got out so Jakob could adjust the seats, making room for everyone. Bits tried to comfort Ange who had worked herself up, thinking the worst.

Drew and Paxton joined them at the car. Drew took Ange in his arms, reassuring her that everything was going to be fine but silently terrified that it wouldn't. Pax and Bits squeezed into the third row then Drew and Ange got it.

"Do you want me to drive?" Jack asked. Jakob shook his head no.

"I need something to do."

The car was silent for the hour-and-ten-minute drive to the hospital, only the occasional sniffle from Ange piercing through the absence of sound.

Once they arrived at the hospital, Jakob pulled up in front of the emergency room doors and dropped everyone off before finding a place to park. Inside, Jack went immediately to the desk, requesting to go back to the treatment area to provide assistance. The nurse buzzed him back. The group found Chance, Waverly, and Cassie with Renaldo and Kasie Cresswell, Rowan's parents, looking anxious in the waiting room. Karl had gone back to the accident scene to relieve the other deputy.

"Thank goodness you all made it here safely," Waverly said as the group shared hugs. "They aren't telling us a thing."

"Jack just went back to see what's going on and help if he can. He will let us know something soon," Paxton said. Jakob joined them.

"Has anyone called Gavin, Owen, or Mom and Dad?" he asked. Everyone shook their heads no.

"I've got it. I will call them now." Jakob was happy to have a task. Sitting in the waiting room not knowing what was happening would make him even more crazy with worry than he already was. He picked up his phone and dialed Gavin.

"On a date here," Gavin said. Jakob could hear music and voices in the background.

"Gavin, there's been an accident."

"Shit, I can't hear you. One second." Jakob could hear Gavin talking to someone and then it got quiet in the background. "Okay, I am outside. What did you say?"

"There's been an accident. Kylie, Brax, and Rowan Cresswell were coming home from the Fall Fest and their car was hit by a train. We are all at the emergency room now. The weather here is crazy."

"Jesus, Jakob! How bad?"

"We don't know anything yet, but it's bad. Jack just went back to get some details and help out if he can."

"Have you called Mom and Dad?"

"No. No one has called Owen either."

"Okay. I will call Owen. You call Mom and Dad. Tell them I am going home then picking up Owen before heading that way."

"Check the weather, Gavin. It's going to take you forever to get here in this ice storm."

"I don't care. We can't just sit here and wait. Flights will be cancelled, so I don't see another alternative."

"I'll call Mom and Dad now and let you know when we hear something from Jack."

"Okay. Talk to you later." Gavin disconnected and ordered an Uber for his date. He went into the restaurant to pay the bill and let her know. Once she was safely in the car and on her way home, he dialed Owen and walked to his own vehicle.

"Hey," Owen answered, distracted by the book he was reading.

"Owen, Kylie and Braxton were in a pretty bad accident tonight. Jakob just called. I am on my way to the house to grab a bag. I will swing by and pick you up in forty-five minutes or so, and we can stop and get Mom and Dad on the way."

"Holy shit, Gavin! Is it bad?"

"No one really knows anything yet. Jack is back with the doctors. Jakob said they would call when they knew more. Evidently we are in for an adventure. There is an ice storm in Collingswood."

"I'll be ready when you get here. Let me know if you hear anything."

Owen immediately dialed Caelan, filling him in on what happened. Caelan was getting in the car and heading towards Barber and would meet them at the hospital. Owen was relieved; he knew he would need the support.

Meanwhile, Jakob was calling his parents.

"Hello?" his mother answered.

"Hey, Mom. Is Dad around?" Jakob tried to sound as normal as possible.

"Sure, sweetheart, one minute. Cord? It's Jakob for you."

"Hi, Jakob." Jakob felt a lump in his throat.

"Hi, Dad." His eyes welled up with tears and his voice broke.

"Son, take a deep breath and tell me what's happened."

Jakob proceeded to repeat the story he felt like he had told a thousand times that evening. He told his father that Gavin and Owen would pick them up soon and that he would be in touch if there was any news. They ended the call. Jakob felt exhausted. He had one last call to make.

"Hello?"

"Hey, baby."

"Jakob," he could hear the relief in her voice, "where are you? How are things?"

"We are all at the hospital now, just waiting. I don't know anything yet. I just needed to hear your voice."

"I'm so glad you called. I was worried. I am still worried. Can I do anything from here?"

"No, we are all about as good as we can be. I will let you know once Jack fills us in."

"Okay. Give everyone my love and let me know if you need anything."

They disconnected Then Shiloh's phone rang.

"Hello?"

"Shiloh, it's Penni. I am so sorry to call so late, but I was hoping that you or Jakob had heard from Jack."

"Oh, Penni. I am so sorry you had to worry. Jack is fine. Jakob's niece and nephew were injured in an accident. All of them are at the hospital and Jack is in with them now. I am sure he forgot to call in all the chaos."

"Oh, no! That's terrible news about his family. I am glad he is okay though. Will you let me know if you hear anything?"

"Of course I will!"

Back at the hospital, the news from Jack wasn't good. Jack sat on the coffee table in front of Rowan's parents.

"Rowan has suffered what we call traumatic cardiac arrest. It occurred from the impact of the steering wheel against his chest and it has caused his heart to stop beating several times. They have taken him to surgery to try to repair the issues." Kasie let out a sob. "It will be a few hours before we know anything."

Jack turned his attention to Drew and Ange. "Braxton suffered spinal trauma. At this time, he is being stabilized so he can rest without moving, without making the injuries worse. He's not breathing on his own right now, so they have him on a ventilator. It's going to be a few days of wait and see before we know anything definitive." Drew felt like he had been punched in the gut.

Jack moved on to Chance and Waverly. "Kylie has a significant traumatic brain injury. There is swelling in her brain and they have taken her to surgery to remove a piece of her skull to make more room. We won't know anything until that swelling goes down." Chance stood and moved to the windows, not wanting to break down in front of his wife, daughter, and the rest of his family.

"They will be in ICU once the surgeries are completed. You all can move up to the waiting room on the fifth floor, and I will update you again once we know more. I am going to go back and see if there is anything else I can help with. The ER is overflowing with injuries from the storm." Jack turned to Jakob. "You okay to update Gavin?" Jakob nodded. He just wished he was calling with better news.

Phone calls were made, and everyone who needed to be updated was contacted. By the time that Gavin, Owen, Beverly, and Cord arrived, there were several inches of snow on the ground, which was quite unusual for the area. Collingswood and the surrounding towns were all but shut down.

Gavin surveyed the waiting room full of his family. Chance was pacing, unable to sit still. Waverly was nose down in her tablet, googling everything she could find about traumatic brain injuries, further freaking herself out with each article she read. Drew was sitting, stoic, while Ange was struggling to pull herself together after another bout of tears. Cassie was asleep, her head resting on Uncle Jakob's leg. Pax and Bits seemed to have set aside their issues for the time being with Elizabeth dosing with her head on his shoulder, his arm firmly around her. Hugs were exchanged and the new arrivals were taken back to see Kylie and Brax. A few hours later, Caelan arrived and set out to comfort Owen and the rest of the family.

It was about fifteen hours after the accident that Shiloh and Penni arrived. Penni had commandeered a cart from the front desk and the two women came into the waiting room with breakfast, snacks, coffee, sodas, books, magazines, pillows, toiletries, cell phone chargers, everything you could think of that you might need for an extended stay at the hospital.

"Baby, what are you doing here? The roads are a mess!" Jakob scolded but he couldn't have been happier to see Shiloh.

"Penni and I couldn't stand sitting at home any longer. We decided to risk the drive so we could bring you guys some supplies and see if there was anything we could do." Jakob kissed her softly on the mouth.

"Thank you for being here."

"There is no where else I would rather be, Jakob." Jakob introduced Penni to Gavin, Owen, and his parents. The women made quick work of distributing supplies and setting up the food. Jack came into the waiting room, looking exhausted. His face brightened when he saw Penni.

"What are you doing here?" he asked with a smile.

"Shiloh and I couldn't take waiting at home, so we made the trip over. We thought you guys might need supplies, food, and moral support." Jack put his arms around her, pulling her close.

"I'm really glad you're here, Pen," he whispered.

The next two days were filled with waiting and worry. There wasn't much change in any of their conditions. Chance, Waverly, Angelica, and Drew kept a constant vigil, rarely leaving the bedsides of their respective children. The rest of the family stayed at the hospital as well, unwilling to leave until they knew something. The weather conditions were improving since the freak storm had moved out, leaving behind a wake of power outages, damaged property, and injured people in its path. Shiloh and Penni were the runners, heading out to get meals, changes of clothes, anything the family requested, and things they didn't even know they needed.

It was in the afternoon of the third day of the agonizing vigil that an update was shared by the Cooke family patriarch. Cord gathered his family into the waiting room to share the news. . .

ACKNOWLEDGEMENTS

A special thanks to my family who supports my crazy writing hobby. To my best friend, Cheryl – thank you for helping me name, develop, and sort out the stories of these seven brothers. To my editor, Lisa – thank you for making this into something better. And finally, thank you to my work family and friends who take such an active role in supporting this part of my life.

The story continues on *The Sordid Road to Rhapsody*, book three in The Roads Collection:

Trey Watson has left his life in Charleston behind, succeeding in a high-profile job at North Essex Hospital in London. While enjoying professional accolades and achievements, Trey continues to find himself at loose ends on the relationship front. He wonders if he will ever find the life and love he truly desires. Trey experiences both personal and professional ups and downs as he navigates *The Sordid Road to Rhapsody*.

The Cooke brothers and their stories continue:

You met Jack Cooke in book one of The Roads Collection, *The Perilous Road to Happiness*. You've met the other six Cooke brothers in *The Precarious Road to Starting Anew*. Follow their lives and the highs and lows of small-town living in this new series, The Cookes of Collingswood. The first book, *A Delicate Strength*, picks up where we last left the Cooke brothers. Join us to continue their stories.